THE GOLD POINT

THE GOLD POINT

AND OTHER STRANGE STORIES

Charles Loring Jackson

COACHWHIP PUBLICATIONS

Landisville, Pennsylvania

The Gold Point and Other Strange Stories, by Charles Loring Jackson
Copyright © 2011 Coachwhip Publications
No claims made on public domain material.
First published 1926.

ISBN 1-61646-085-7
ISBN-13 978-1-61646-085-3

   Cover: Tropical island © Ben Goode

CoachwhipBooks.com

CONTENTS

The Gold Point

I first met Alonzo Fortescue when I went up to X— for my college entrance exams. I had scraped acquaintance with some of the X— high school boys, and we were standing in the campus talking over our luck, when one of them said:

"Have any of you fellows heard from Alonzo Fortescue?"

"Alonzo Fortescue!" said I. "What a name!"

"Look out! There he is."

And then I saw another boy had joined us, but he was the very last to have such a romantic name. He was short and insignificant with hair a carroty red, a plain freckled face, pale blue eyes, and no eyebrows. The worst of it was he must have heard me, as he gave me a look of venomous hate, which was very queer on such a face.

Next fall after College began I made a point of going to see every one of my classmates, but put off my call on Alonzo Fortescue till the very last, as I barely knew him. There was not much chance of knowing him, as he did not go out for athletics, made no calls, and even cut the religious meetings. Of course, he was in none of the Freshman Societies, and, as he was no sort of a scholar, he seemed to me the most insignificant man in the class. Then, too, he was so grumpy and disagreeable that I don't think any of the boys knew him well.

When I made my call at last, there was no answer to my knock, so I pushed the door open, but he was not at home. As I was turning to go, I caught sight of a large book bound in leather and with brass clasps lying open on the table, and wondered what Alonzo could be doing with a book like that, wondered still more when I found it was in Latin and such hard Latin, that I did not see how he could read it, as he was no good in Latin. Why! It took even me some time to spell out enough to find it was a book on magic! Just as I had found this out, Alonzo came home, and took my chaff about magic so very unpleasantly, that I cut my call as short as possible.

Of course, this was too good a story to keep to myself. The boys all laughed at the idea of Alonzo Fortescue studying magic, and adopted with enthusiasm my nickname for him—the sorcerer.

One day, near the middle of the winter, when I was doing my regular afternoon ex in the gym, Alonzo Fortescue came in. I was surprised, as I had never seen him there before, and I was nearly knocked flat when he came up to me.

"Hullo! Sorcerer!" said I. "Lost your way?"

Instead of flying off the handle, as he usually did, he answered pleasantly:

"No! You see I am not getting exercise enough, and so I thought I would come and work with you, if you don't mind. How about the fencing-room?"

The fencing-room was a hall above the gym intended for fencing, but, as no one in the college fenced, it had come to be used by boys who wanted to exercise away from the racket of the main gym. I had no objection, so I shouldered my heavy Indian club, and was a good deal amused to see Alonzo pick out the lightest dumbbells in the whole place.

When we got upstairs, I began exercising at once, as the fencing-room was far from warm; but Alonzo stayed some time at the doors, and, after he had joined me, instead of beginning to exercise said:

"Well! Goodbye."

"What!" said I, "going already?"

"Yes!" he answered, "I am going, but you will stay."

And he went. I could not help laughing and saying to myself:

"What a queer fish the old sorcerer is!"

So I finished my regular ex alone, and then, as it was nearly time for afternoon class, started to go downstairs, and hit the swinging doors a good solid whack, but they did not move, which was queer, as generally they swung open at a touch. When I pushed them, they did not stir, and so I punched them as hard as I could, but only jarred my arm, as if I had struck a solid wall.

I now remembered Alonzo Fortescue had been monkeying with them (curse him!), and thought he might have wedged them on the outside, but peeping through the crack nearly an inch wide, which ran all round each of them, I could see no wedge or bar, and it seemed impossible they could have been made so fast without showing what held them. The hinges, too, which were on my side, were all right.

Next I thought perhaps the doors might open inward, although I was certain I had seen them swing both ways, and sure enough, my pulling did not move them any more than my pushing.

The bell now rang for afternoon class, and, thoroughly desperate, I charged the doors using my heavy Indian club as a battering-ram, but they were solid as a rock, and clean knocked out, I slumped down upon the bench that ran around the room, and lost the recitation.

For a long time I sat there trying to puzzle out how the doors could have been fastened so firmly, when usually even a gentle breeze set them swinging, until I realized with a start it was nearly time for evening prayers, and, if I missed them, I should be in a mess. Was there no way of getting out? The doors were light wooden frames covered on each side with green enamel cloth, so, if I only had my knife, I could cut through the cloth inside the frame, and, reaching out, pull away the bar, or, whatever it was. Then I saw my Indian club would do as well, and struck the flimsy cloth with it a lot of blows hard enough to shiver a thick plank, but it might have been solid iron, for I did not even dent it.

Now I began to be frightened, as it dawned upon me that it might not be a natural obstacle that held me in, but that idea was too absurd. So I dropped it at once, and went back to battering at the doors, for prayers were now very near. No use! I lost evening prayers and supper too, although this troubled me little, as I was too excited and worried to feel hungry.

Later I heard the janitor unlocking the gym for the evening, and presently coming upstairs to light the gas in the fencing-room. This was a joyful sound, as he would clear away whatever was holding the doors, and put an end to this stupid practical joke of Alonzo's, which had proved so far from a joke for me.

When he reached the doors, they swung open as easily as usual, and I sprang from the bench, and ran to get out, but, when I pushed them, and then flung my whole weight against them, they did not stir, and before I had got over the frightful shock this gave me, Peter, the janitor, had finished his lighting, and gone, leaving the doors swinging. I was at them in an instant, but as I reached them, they became fixed and nothing I could do would move them.

This was too much! It could be nothing natural that stopped me, and let others pass, and the horror of this unnatural, invisible, irresistible something nearly drove me out of my head. I cowered on the bench as far from the terrible doors as I could get, trembling and shivering, until I became half dazed with the horror of it.

After an hour or so the doors swung open, and two Upper classmen came in to exercise. I had not tried to speak to Peter, because, although I was in a bad fix, it was too absurd, but now I was long past minding that, and I ran up to the two men and begged them to help me out, but to my bitter disappointment they took no notice of me, and I could not make them see me, or hear me asking for help.

When I found I could not make myself seen or heard, I was more frightened than before, but I dared not give way, as I needed all my wits to plan for my escape, when the upper classmen left the room, supposing they, like Peter, were able to get out. So I planted myself close to the doors, that I might slip out with them, but, although I was right on their heels, the doors pushed me back, and, when I flung myself against them, did not budge. This was too much! I screamed and shouted for help at the top of my lungs, but no one paid any attention to me, although I could hear distinctly even the little noises from the main gym.

No other students came to exercise, and the evening dragged wearily away, until at last Peter came to put out the lights. Then I threw myself in his way, and begged him to help me, but he neither saw nor heard me, and, when I tried to seize him by the sleeve, my hand slipped down over an invisible, smooth, impenetrable barrier. Then, as he could not walk through me, I stood right in his way, but he turned out to avoid me with a puzzled look on his jolly face, which showed he was wondering why he had done it.

This time I was bound not to lose the chance of getting through the doors, so I stood against one of them, and, as Peter pushed it open actually stepped into the entry, but instantly it swung back with such a tremendous blow that it knocked me almost into the middle of the room, and, before I could get to my feet, Peter had gone, and after him the doors flapped to and fro longer than usual, as if they were jeering at me.

As he turned out the entry light, and left me in the dark, the terror of the doors seemed to crush me, and I longed for even the faintest gleam of light. Anything rather than the threat of those hidden doors!

"Oh! If I could only see them!" I thought.

So it was an unspeakable relief, when later the moon shone into the fencing-room, and, better still, it made me think I might get out through a window. After a hard climb I managed to reach one of the beams of the open roof, from which I could look out of a window, but one look was enough. The roof sloped steeply down from it, and was covered with a glare of icy snow that glistened in the moonlight. An attempt in this way meant certain death.

The moonlight encouraged me to try the doors again, but I could not stir them, and was imprisoned for the night.

It was a terrible night. The fencing-room had been so cold in the early evening, that I had to exercise frequently to keep any warmth in me, but, as the furnace died down, a deadly chill settled on it, which I could fight off only by the hardest sort of exercise, and when tired out I stopped to rest, I began to freeze long before

I was ready to begin again. By the time the night was half over my arms were too tired to use my Indian club, and instead I took to running, until my legs gave out too, and so the long night wore away.

The moonlight, which at first had seemed such a friend, now turned against me, for the faint half light made the doors seem more mysterious, and so even more terrible than when I could not see them distinctly; and I longed for darkness again, but I was wrong, as, after some clouds blotted out the moon, I found the pitchy blackness the worst of all.

And then it seemed as if time had stopped.

Would the night never end?

I did not know a night could be so long, and this waiting and waiting was one of the greatest trials of this dreadful time.

I tell you, I was glad to see the first gray on the eastern windows; and, when the day had fairly come, the thought of prayers drove me to the doors once more, but they stood just as fast as ever, and I lost prayers and breakfast, too, and by this time I was hungry.

Some time later when I heard Peter shaking out the furnace, I started for another desperate try at the doors, and, as I was crossing the room to them, my eye was caught by something glistening on the floor, which I picked up, and found that it was a little triangle of yellow metal. I put it in the pocket of my pants, and threw myself against the doors with all my might, when they yielded to the first touch, and I was thrown sprawling my whole length—but outside! Yes! Really outside! As I scrambled to my feet, the doors were swinging madly, but I did not stop to examine them. Instead I ran down the stairs and across the snowy campus in my thin gym clothes, and did not feel safe, till I had reached my room.

There I devoured ravenously some crackers I was lucky enough to have, tumbled into bed just as I was, and slept like a log till nearly dinner time.

As I got out of my gym clothes for dinner, something scratched my finger, when I was changing my handkerchief from one suit to the other, and turned out to be the curious triangle of metal I had picked up in the fencing-room. Now that I examined it carefully it was even queerer than I thought at first. It was an inch long and three-quarters of an inch wide at the base. The metal, which was thick enough to be stiff, looked like gold, and was entirely covered with a design made by a continuous slender line twisting and turning in the most complicated way. I could not make out whether it was only an ornamental arabesque, or an inscription in some language I did not know. It had evidently been cut in the metal with a fine sharp tool, and then filled with a red transparent paint. I could not make out what this strange thing was, although I puzzled over it for some time, and at last put it into my vest pocket, and went to dinner where I tried not to show how ravenous I was.

At afternoon class I fell perfectly flat, as I had been too tired and excited to study. I was not surprised, therefore, when I was summoned to appear before the faculty. Prexy asked me not un-kindly, if I could give any explanation of my absences, but, when I began to tell my experience in the fencing-room, his face hard-ened, and I saw that not one of the faculty believed my story, and that every word I said increased their feeling against me. Then I took refuge in silence, and did not open my lips again for all their questions.

The next day when I went up to learn my fate, Prexy told me that, although I deserved a severe punishment, the faculty had decided in consideration of my perfect record in the past to let me off with a reprimand, but I must understand any repetition of such behaviour would lead to most serious consequences.

As I started for my room, thinking how lucky I was to get off so easily, I saw Alonzo Fortescue coming along the path toward me, and I am not ashamed to say that I climbed over the high pile of snow on the side of the path, and ploughed through the drift be-yond, although it was a foot deep, rather than meet him face to face. He watched me with a hateful sneer, and I hurried back to my room a good deal shaken by this meeting.

I now settled down to study with a will, as I had all my back work to makeup. But suddenly I sprang from my seat, ran to the door, locked it, bolted it, piled all my heaviest furniture against it, and then cowered against the furthest wall, for I felt *it* coming. *It* was still only half way across the campus, but I knew *it* was coming for me, and, as I felt *it* coming nearer and nearer, I grew more and more frightened.

Now *it* was entering the building, now on the stairs, and now I tried to shrink through the wall as *it* reached my room. Before *it* the door flew from its bolts and hinges, scattering my barricade in all directions, and *it* came in!

On! On *it* came toward me! Nearer and nearer! I was lost. . . . And then something bright flashed out, and quivered in the air before me, and *it* went,—yes! *it* went!

The idea of facing *it* again was too much for me, so I hurried some clothes into my grip, and started to catch the evening train for home. As I reached the depot, I came face to face with Alonzo Fortescue, who was standing on the platform. He grinned down at me with his hateful sneer.

"Oh!" said he. "Running away are you? Well! I will set the gold point on you!"

I did not know what he meant, but it frightened me all the more, and I was much relieved to see him turn off into the gathering dusk, as I went into the waiting-room to buy my ticket.

When the train came, he was nowhere in sight, and I was the only passenger to get in, so I settled down in my seat with the comfortable thought that every turn of the wheels was taking me further from Alonzo Fortescue. As I thought this, I glanced out of the window, and—there he was running along beside the train!

"We shall soon leave him behind," I thought.

But, no! He still ran on beside us, even after the train had gathered full speed, and, as he ran, he kept feeling in his vest pockets, as if he had lost something. Presently we came to a thick belt of woods, and I thought:

"Now we shall get rid of him."

But again I was wrong, for he ran up over the trees, and along their tops as easily as he had on the level ground, and all the time he was searching in his vest pockets.

In this way he ran beside the train for some ten miles, and then I saw him suddenly throw his arms above his head, when the car left the rails, and rolled over and over down a steep embankment, until it lit at the bottom with a crash.

When I pulled myself together, I found I was lying among the ruins, pinned down by a great beam, so that I could not move; I tried and tried to push it off, but did not stir it, as it was wedged fast at each end.

By the time I had found I could not get free without help, the unhurt passengers began to break into the car to rescue us, and soon were taking out the people from the other end, so that I waited quietly for my turn. But this quiet did not last long. The stove, as it rolled over and over, had scattered its burning coals among the splintered woodwork, which caught fire, and almost at once was in a light blaze.

It was now a race between the flames and the rescuing party. How they worked! But would they reach me in time? For I lay at the end of the car furthest from the hole through which the injured were carried to safety, and the flames were coming terribly fast. Man after man was taken out, until my turn came, and the fire was not yet upon me. Then, as one of the rescuers lifted the last man before me out of the car, he said with a sigh of relief,

"There! That makes all. Every one is out."

"No! No!" I screamed, "I am left. Save me! Save me! Help! Help! Help!"

But no one heard me, and I was left to my fate. And what a fate! To lie pinned there, as the flames came careering nearer and nearer, and then to burn!

I struggled furiously, desperately to push off the beam, but I only bruised my hands, and exhausted my strength. I screamed at the top of my lungs, but it was to deaf ears. Alonzo had seen to that, and all the time the flames were rushing nearer.

Here I must have fainted, as I have no remembrance of the fire reaching me, but I suddenly came to myself to find it roaring all about me. Even the beam that held me down was blazing.

Then I noticed a strange thing.

I felt no heat!

The beam was burning fiercely, where it lay across my chest, but my coat was not even scorched, and I felt no more than a pleasant warmth from that blaze, or from the rest of the fire, which was pressing upon me on every side. When a fierce spurt of flame blew against my bare hand, so far from burning, it felt only as if I had been stroked with something softer than the softest feather.

While I was wondering what this could mean, the beam was blazing merrily, and I lay placidly watching it, until it was so nearly burned through, that I snapped it in halves easily, and, throwing aside the ends sprang to my feet, and walked out to safety through the wall of the car, which dropped in glowing ruins as I reached it.

Far enough off to avoid the terrible heat a little crowd was watching the fire, and, as I stepped out of this raging furnace, a great cry of astonishment went up, followed by a hush even more impressive. But when they took it in that I was really alive, they broke into wild cheering. All the same, they could not believe their eyes, until they had gathered round me, felt me all over, and found that I was not only alive but uninjured, and more wonderful still my clothes were not scorched, and showed not even the faintest smell of fire.

In the midst of their questions and congratulations I noticed that a man left the edge of the crowd, and walked moodily away. It was Alonzo Fortescue.

*   *   *   *   *

When I reached home I told my father that I could not stay at college, and, when he pressed me for my reasons, remembering my experience with the faculty, I took refuge in silence. For a day, or two he argued the matter with me, and grew so angry at my silence, that I think he would have sent me back to X—, if a letter had not arrived from Prexy advising him to give me a rest for some time. From what he told me, and did not, I came to the conclusion that Prexy thought I was somewhat off my head.

Certainly I was far from well. I was so used up that I could hardly drag myself from my bed to the couch, and besides I felt a dreadful oppression, or rather I should call it pressure, sometimes in one part of my body, sometimes in another, and, worst of all, I had occasionally, either in my head, or chest, stinging pains so fierce that I could hardly bear them.

The doctor was sent for, but the tonic and complete rest that he ordered, did me no good, and I continued to run downhill very fast.

After I had been at home about a week, one day aimlessly searching my pockets I came across the metal triangle, which I had picked up in the fencing-room; (this was the first time I had worn that vest since I came from X—). As I was looking at it, and wondering what it could be, and if it had any use, one of my eyelids itched, and I scratched it with the point of the triangle. Instantly I found myself looking into Alonzo Fortescue's room in the college dormitory twenty miles away. The book of magic lay open on the table, and upon it was sitting a little wax doll, which looked like me in a distant grotesque way. Alonzo, in one corner of the room, was working with a pair of long wooden tongs in an open packing case, from which came a strange rattling noise that I could not understand, until presently he drew out of it a live rattlesnake, which he had seized by the neck, and carried the beast squirming violently below the tongs, or coiling about them, to the book of magic, and held it toward the doll, when it wound itself around and around the little figure, and at once I felt with the deepest loathing the slimy coils of the reptile pressing upon my body, and its scales grating against my flesh.

He now began striking the snake on its head with the tongs, until rattling fiercely it reared itself, and drove its fangs deep into the head of the waxen image, and the fearful stinging pang, which shot through my brain, threw me fainting on the floor.

When I came to myself, I found they had put me to bed, and I did not try to get up, for the pain was still very severe, though less terrible than at first, and, what was nearly as bad, I knew that the venomous reptile was still coiled about my body, as I could feel the creeping movement of its scales and the occasional loosening and tightening of its grip.

At first the feeling that this loathsome beast was wound about me was frightfully repulsive, but, as the afternoon wore on, this horror faded away; and by evening I found myself absolutely taking an evil pleasure in it, and realized with a shock that the bestial nature of the serpent was taking possession of me. I fought against it with all my strength, but it was too much for me, and, as the night went on, I felt my human nature driven out by the venomous, malignant serpent nature, until by midnight its victory was complete, and with all human feeling crushed out my one thought was vengeance on Alonzo Fortescue for all that he had made me suffer.

I sprang from my bed and, seizing the point, impressed my commands upon it, when instantly I was flying through the air with such speed that in a few seconds I found myself floating outside Alonzo Fortescue's room twenty miles away in X—.

And now the point sprang from my hand, and passing into his room began to move to and fro along the wall above his bed, cutting through the solid masonry, as it went, so that its path was marked by a bright, somewhat waving line, where the light from inside shone through.

After it had traversed the wall for some time, cutting through it these close-set bright wavering lines running side by side over a large space, it passed out of the building, and turning its point toward the weakened brickwork poured forth a furious blast, before which the wall fell with a tremendous crash, and I woke up in my bed at home.

The next morning my headache had subsided to a distant grumbling, and, what was quite as great a relief, I was free from the loathsome clutch of the serpent, and picked up so rapidly that by evening I felt quite myself again.

When I thought over the night in the clear sensible light of day, I decided the whole had been only a wonderfully vivid dream, but on Saturday the following paragraph in the county newspaper proved I was wrong:

"Mysterious Fatality"

"We regret to announce an inexplicable occurrence, which resulted in the passing away of one of the most popular and brilliant members of the freshman class at the College—A. Fortescue of this municipality. On Tuesday night he retired to rest, anticipating no evil, but the following morning it was ascertained that a considerable portion of the wall of the college dormitory, in which he resided, had been precipitated upon his bed, crushing him beneath its terrific impact. Thus in the midst of life we are in death!

"The college authorities are investigating the sad accident, but at the hour of going to press assured a representative of *The Harbinger* that, as yet, no explanation had been arrived at for this mysterious weakening of the masonry in this portion of the edifice, especially as the remainder of the structure retained its pristine solidity.

"On Thursday at a meeting of the Freshman Class the following resolutions received unanimous approval:—

"*Whereas*, it has pleased a Merciful Providence in its all wise dispensations to remove our beloved associate and classmate, Alonzo Fortescue, from this mundane sphere,

"*Resolved*, that in him we deplore the loss of one of the brightest ornaments of our Class, who had endeared himself to all of them by his qualities of mind and heart. A brilliant scholar, a devoted friend, whose career, if it had not been brought to this premature termination, would certainly have made a mark in the world.

"Resolved, that a copy of these *Resolutions* be sent to his afflicted family, and that they be published in *The Harbinger*."

It was no dream then! The death of Alonzo Fortescue lay at my door! At first I was crushed by this conviction. A murderer! I shuddered at myself! But a calmer view of the facts showed me I had nothing to regret. It was not I who had killed him, but the malignant serpent nature, which he, himself, had instilled into me, and against which I had struggled with all my strength. Besides, a man may always fight for his life, and in this case it was his life or mine, as I knew well that those Resolutions would have been headed by my name, instead of Alonzo Fortescue's, if it had not been for the Gold Point.

The Moth
A Sequel to the Gold Point

The lucky owner of such a powerful talisman as the Gold Point had a comfortable and easy time of it, for even before the end of his freshman year Edgar Anston had found study was entirely unnecessary. To transfer the whole contents of a book to his mind, he had simply to rub the point against his forehead, after he had scratched the outside of the book with it. This left him all the time and energy his class-mates gave to study to use for other things, and soon he became first at once in his studies, in the debating society, in athletics, in the missionary meetings, and in all the other college activities.

These successes in so many different fields made him the wonder of his class, and, although they brought him some enemies, his attractive personality and pleasant manners gave him still more friends, so that he was admitted to be the most popular man in his class, and even those who disliked him, were proud of the credit his achievements brought to the class and the college.

As his senior year drew to its close bets were freely made on the winner of the valedictory. In any other class Anston would have been certain of this honor, but in his there was a man named Boyne, a typical first scholar, who lived only for study, and with his wonderful memory and intellect pushed Anston hard.

Throughout the year they ran neck and neck, until at last the decision hung on the result of the examination in ethics. Here Anston felt entirely safe, as he was so much interested in the subject that for the first three recitations he had studied the lessons

21

like any one else, and after this transferred the subject-matter to his mind by means of the gold point, only because the baseball season had begun, and he needed all his time for practice.

So the morning of the examination found him full of confidence. As he was dressing a small, gray moth flew against him, and, when he brushed it away, returned to the charge over and over again in the most strangely persistent way behaving, in fact, more like a mosquito than one of those insignificant common moths.

Before the examination he made assurance doubly sure by once more scratching the book on ethics with the gold point, and then drawing it across his forehead, and took his place in the examination room with the feeling of a conqueror; but, when he settled down to work, to his dismay he found that the whole subject had dropped out of his head with the exception of the three lessons, which he had studied, and of these he had only a somewhat vague remembrance. The result was a disastrous failure, and Boyne carried off the valedictory.

It was Anston's first defeat, and he took it very much to heart. In fact, he managed to get through the salutatory only because he was determined to show himself a good sport.

All through college, like all his classmates, he had been exposed to increasing pressure from the authorities to go into foreign missions, but had not yielded in the least, as it was the life of all others which he most detested; and on graduation he decided to try his luck in New York, but before settling down he treated himself to a last vacation at one of the resorts on the coast of Maine, then a quiet simple place far removed from the height of fashion it has since reached. His principal reason for choosing this place for his summer was that Ella Traft was going there from X—, and he had been her devoted slave during his last two years in college.

For the first month his vacation was all that he had hoped, but with August came a Mr. Van Mahder from New York, and this much older man, with his prestige of wealth and position, swept Ella entirely off her feet. Anston was certain that but for this unfair handicap he could have held his own, and at last, stung by Van

Mahder's superior air and veiled sneers, he called on the gold point to clear this rival out of his way.

The plan suggested by the point was that Ella's little dog Fidele—adored by its mistress, but detested by all the rest of the world—should be found by her hung from a tree in a noose made from strips of Van Mahder's handkerchief.

A picnic a few days later gave an excellent opportunity for carrying out the plot, and, as luncheon approached, Anston succeeded in touching Fidele's neck and Van Mahder's hand with the point, so he was not surprised, when, a few minutes later, Ella sent Mr. Van Mahder to the brook for water, and the dog ran off into the woods in the same direction.

He meanwhile, was watching the ladies arrange the luncheon, and presently they sent him to the brook for some ferns to decorate the table cloth. As he did not bring nearly enough, the whole party, including Van Mahder, who by this time had come with the water, strolled toward the brook for more.

After a few steps a frantic rustling in the bushes startled them and there was Fidele kicking and struggling in a noose made of a handkerchief torn into strips. Ella ran screaming to the rescue, and tore the little brute free, unhurt except for the fright. The point had done its work well, as the owner's name stood out on the handkerchief so conspicuously that Ella pounced on it at once, and Anston, who had prudently kept in the background, smiled to himself at the thought of the coming explosion, when, to his utter astonishment, she came flying at him and shook the rags in his face.

"You! You did it! How could you? Poor little Fidele! He would not hurt a fly, and you—"

Here she broke down, and Anston to his horrified bewilderment read his own name on the handkerchief.

What did it mean? How could the point have failed him? By what terrible mistake had it used his handkerchief instead of Van Mahder's? But there was no time for such questions, for the other guests, as soon as they had taken in the situation, burst into a torrent of abuse of one who would kill a poor innocent dog, and, worse

still, Ella's dog! No words were bad enough for him. In fact, some
of the men led by Van Mahder, who made the most of this opening, even proposed to duck him in the brook, and became so threatening that he slipped off into the woods, and made his way home-
wards with no cheering thoughts for company on his long, dreary
walk. He was too wretched even to feel the loss of his dinner.

After plodding on wearily for some two hours he had nearly
reached the village, when he heard the buckboard coming up behind him, and, as he had no stomach for another encounter with
the picnickers, hid in the bushes by the side of the road, from which
he could see without being seen. The noise of talk and laughter, as
they rattled past, showed the incident had not dashed the spirits
of the party. Ella was on the back seat with the rescued Fidele in
her lap, who seemed none the worse, except that he was even more
pop-eyed than usual. Beside her sat Van Mahder leaning over her
with an air of ownership, which he took no pains to conceal, and
which was gall and bitterness to Anston.

After they were out of sight, he stole from his hiding place, and,
sneaking into the village luckily without being noticed, locked himself into his room, until it was time for the evening boat, which
under cover of the darkness he was able to board without meeting
any one he knew. There was nothing else to do, for after this catas-
trophe he could not even think of staying at the hotel.

As it was still early in the season, he could get a stateroom to
himself, and at once shut himself into it for fear of meeting some
acquaintance. Here, as he got over his excitement and disappointment enough to think, he was overwhelmed with astonishment.

What did it mean?

The gold point had always served him well before.

It had never failed him, except—yes! Except in that ethics examination, and, as his mind ran back to that he remembered how
on that morning, while he was dressing, a gray moth had flown
against him, and kept on persistently flying at him over and over
again, in spite of all his efforts to brush it away. Why did this trifle
come back to him now so vividly? And then it rushed into his mind
that the very same thing had happened this morning.

The moth was larger than before, nearly twice as big, but gray and not to be brushed off. Was it a mere coincidence? Or had this moth something to do with the failure of the point? Think as he would, he could find no answer to these questions.

By eleven he had become somewhat resigned to the inevitable, and decided a cigar on deck in the moonlight would quiet his nerves, and help him go to sleep, and it would be safe enough, as at this time all the other passengers would be in their bunks, but he had not taken two turns on deck when he was hailed by one of the men who had been at the picnic.

"Hullo, Anston!" he shouted. "You did put your foot in it! Whatever made you meddle with that dirty little beast?"

"Dry up!"

"But tell me, how the devil did you dare touch the light of the fair Ella's eyes? I thought you were rather gone there."

"Dry up, I say!"

"Don't get mad! If you had only done for him, we should have given you a vote of thanks, but with the fair Ella by, we all had to take her side."

"Dry up. Darn you!"

"Well anyway, it's all settled. What? Haven't you heard? No? Her engagement to Van Mahder came out, before we got into the buckboard. Going to bed? Better finish your cigar. Well! So long then!"

For the first three years of his stay in New York Anston worked hard and with fair success in a place, he had been lucky enough to get. During this time he heard occasionally of Ella Van Mahder, for in the fast and showy Van Mahder set she out-heroded Herod so completely that news of her exploits spread all over the city, even to the obscure circle in which Anston moved; and, as escapade followed escapade, he began to thank the power, whatever it was, which had rescued him from what he had hoped would be his greatest happiness.

In his fourth or fifth year the whirlpool of the stock exchange began to suck him in. At first he plunged timidly and with slight

success, but one evening, while reading the financial news, he felt
a hot almost burning sensation in his side, which presently he
traced to the gold point in his waistcoat pocket. Taking it out he
found it nearly too hot to hold, and laid it on the newspaper to
cool. Then the letters in the financial article seemed to dance before his eyes; and in a few seconds after they had settled down, he
found, to his intense surprise, he was reading the news not of that
day, but of the next, and on the following evening this had proved
correct to the minutest detail. Then once more he laid the gold
point on the financial news, and again there was the short wavering of the letters followed by the shifting of the date giving the
news twenty-four hours ahead and, as before, this proved absolutely true.

After this experiment had succeeded several times, he ventured
a little money on one of the point's prophecies with an entirely
satisfactory result, and a second attempt going quite as well he
took courage, and began to use the gold point in working the market.

Once sure of his ground he plunged into huge operations, and,
as he was always successful, became the talk of the street, and the
papers were soon full of the "Meteor of Wall Street," as he was
called.

To do him justice the excitement of victory attracted him even
more than the money he made, large as these sums were, but, as
these excitements became every day affairs, he began to long for
something livelier than following the natural fluctuations of the
market, and made some modest experiments in changing prices
by means of the gold point, which proved that he could raise, or
lower any stock at will.

Now with the market completely at his mercy he tried to use
his power as dictator with a certain amount of discretion, but the
consciousness of it was too intoxicating, and he could not always
resist the temptation of startling the world by most astonishing
fluctuations, and especially after reading an article, in which some
financial pundit tried to explain the strange and abnormal variations of the market, he would impress his commands on the gold

point, and send the stocks flying in ways more utterly crazy than anything he had attempted before.

By this time he had become a national figure, and his judgment (save the mark!), his daring, and above all, his wealth were trumpeted in every part of the country.

At last, however, he had had enough of even such excitements, so he arranged a great stroke, which should at once put the copestone on his already colossal fortune, and mark his retirement from speculation. With this in view, he bought heavily a number of comparatively worthless stocks, and then issued his orders to the gold point to drive them up enough to give him an enormous profit; and, after all these arrangements for the next day were finished, went to bed, and fell asleep full of visions of triumph.

On the morning of his great day he began to dress with the gayest expectations.

And then a moth came flying at him.

A large gray moth, which could not be brushed away. And it was March! March! When no moths fly! As he realized this, the last shred of hope fell from him.

He could not tell how he managed to get into the rest of his clothes. Breakfast was not for him, and he hurried downtown feverish for news; but, before he had turned into Wall Street, he met one of his rivals and one look at his face was enough, so that he did not need the gleeful shout of

"All down! Bottom out of every damn one of them!"

to tell him he was irretrievably ruined. Down he slumped upon the curb, and, in spite of the jeers of the passers-by, sat there hunched up, with his face buried in his hands for several minutes, before he could pull himself together enough to go home.

When at last he felt equal to looking over the wreck, he found that the power acting against him had taken a malicious pleasure in destroying every arrangement he had made with the help of the gold point. His great fortune had vanished, and he felt very grateful that he had not been left entirely penniless.

For a year or so he went away from New York, and dropped out of sight, until the scandal of his fall had worn itself out. During this retirement he had much time for thought, and it was borne in on him that in all the cases, where the gold point had failed, he was using it for his selfish advantage, and in ways which were questionable, to say the least. He resolved, therefore, to devote himself in the future to some great work for the good of others, and to use the point only for this, if he used it at all, and never in any way that would be mean or unworthy.

When he thought over the various kinds of public work, he was attracted at once by the cause of temperance (this was years before the day of national prohibition), and determined to devote his life to this glorious struggle for the good of the world. Accordingly, he launched out as a temperance orator and reformer with great and instant success. He was never quite sure whether his glowing and convincing oratory was all his own, or reinforced by the power of the gold point, if not in some measure imparted to him by it, but he was certain that knowingly he had never called on it for such help.

Years passed and his work prospered so that he became the leading figure among temperance reformers, and yet, when at the first approach of age he thought over his work as a whole, he was overwhelmed with bitter discouragement. His onslaughts, which seemed so effective at the time, now, when looked at against the vast amount still to be done, dwindled to almost nothing. They might, it was true, lead to real victories, if followed up, but who was there to follow them up? His day would soon be over, and among his colleagues and disciples there was not one who had the incisive energy needed to carry on the work. If only his life could be lengthened, a mortal blow could be dealt this terrible evil, but if in a few years he must give up, all his work would go for nothing, and the world fall back again into the clutches of drink.

These thoughts were pressing on his mind one winter evening, as he lay upon the couch before a blazing fire in his study, when he heard a child crying in the darkness outside, and going to the door found a fine sturdy baby lying in a basket, abandoned on the door-step. After he had found no message, or clue of any sort upon the child, he put it, basket and all, upon the table to wait until his housekeeper came home, as she would know what to do for it.

As he lay down again before the fire, his gloomy thoughts about the failure of his work came upon him with even greater force after this interruption, and then he saw, or perhaps it was suggested to him by the gold point, that here was the solution of all his troubles. With the help of the point he could draw forth the life of this infant, and by drinking it reinforce his failing powers with all this overflowing energy, and with these added years of vigorous work he would be able to crush the demon of drink. Had not this foundling been sent to him at the very moment, when the failure of his strength threatened to wreck his great work for Humanity? Surely the coincidence had a deeper meaning, and Heaven itself pointed the way to saving the Human Race.

No sooner planned than done. He sprang up, placed a glass on the table by the basket, and then drawing the gold point from his pocket impressed his commands upon it. It flew from his hand, and hung in the air with its sharp end toward the child, its blunt one toward the glass. Then it put forth all its power. It positively quivered with its excess of energy, but for some minutes, that seemed like hours, nothing happened. At last—Ping! It was the sound of a drop falling sharply into the glass. Then after a long pause, another; and soon they began to come faster, dropping at last in a steady stream, until the glass was nearly half full of a liquid.

But was it a liquid? This something, which seemed trying to fly out of the glass, and was held back only by a semi-conscious determination to stay there. Its surface was not tranquil and smooth, but miniature waves continually chased one another over it, or sometimes the whole liquid would rise up unsupported from the middle of the glass, or climb one side of it, and, just as it was about to pour over the edge, it would be drawn back by a change of plan, for it was impossible to deny reason and will to this strange something.

Its color was reddish white, but was not constant. At times it would throw forth gleams like vivid flame, or in the hollows of the waves it would glow like hot iron, or more sombrely with the lurid crimson of clotted blood. Then again, all these fiercer shades would be dashed out of it, and the whole would gleam with intense blushing white light.

When the point began its attack upon the child, he stirred uneasily in his sleep, and, when the first drop fell in the glass, uttered a little troubled cry, but only one, as after that he sank into too deep a trance, or sleep. His eyes seemed to sink into his head, his skin grew waxen, and his breathing, at first more measured, became slower and slower, until at last it fell to one labored breath in several seconds.

Meanwhile Anston lay on the couch eagerly watching the life of the baby dropping into the glass, and thinking with triumph of the moment, when by making this life his own he would be equipped for a victorious fight for Humanity.

And then a huge gray moth flew against him.

It was his old enemy, though so much larger, and it was midwinter!

As it flew but sluggishly, he saw a chance of vengeance for all the evil it had done him. With a violent clutch he grasped it, and threw it into the midst of the flames, where it caught fire, swelled up, opening out like a book to twice its first size, and sailing up to the mouth of the chimney clung to the fire-back a great gray skull.

Then with stunning force the truth fell on him. This was murder!

He sprang from the couch, and, as he looked at the child, its breathing dropped to a mere convulsive flutter just sinking into quiet.

Was he too late?

He threw himself on the point, turned it end for end, and then hung over the table with his eyes glued on the pallid face of the baby.

Was he too late?

There was an endless pause; and then the feeble flutter came again, and after another eternity yet again, and—thank Heaven!—it was a little stronger, unless his fierce desire cheated him.

But soon doubt ended, as each breath was plainly stronger and deeper than the last, and—yes!—they were certainly nearer together.

When the point had drawn nearly half of the life out of the glass back to the child, and its breathing was once more regular and easy, the rush of his thankfulness and relief was almost too much for him. He had been saved. Thank Heaven!—but from the very jaws of destruction.

Then, as the last of the liquid vanished from the glass, and the child's life once more flowed in a brimming stream, he was overcome with loathing for himself. How could he have been betrayed into such a crime? And his motives too—had they really been so fine and noble? For now, mixed with his zeal for the service of Humanity, he grew aware of a large alloy of ambition and longing for his own glory. Yes! There was reason that he should shudder at himself.

In the dreary days that followed one thought began to obscure everything else—Expiation! What could he do to atone for his great sin? And gradually and unwillingly the decision forced itself upon him that the only way he could do this was by becoming a foreign missionary. Here were vast opportunities for usefulness with no rewarding glory, and he could find no more severe penance than taking up this life, which of all others he most detested.

The foundling, indeed, might have interfered with this plan, but his housekeeper, while caring for the baby during his time of doubt, had become so fond of it that she was eager to adopt it. So, after he had settled on the child enough of the remains of his fortune to make it comfortable for life, the path was clear before him.

All the necessary preparations being made, he called upon the point to transport him to one of the most remote parts of Central Africa, and, after it had made him familiar with the language of the natives, he entered on the labors of his mission.

When he saw the impression that his appearance without even a single porter made on these savages, he was sorely tempted to call on the point for a few miracles to help his teaching, but he resisted this temptation, and, if the gold point helped his preaching it was without direction, or even intention on his part.

And his labors prospered exceedingly. The man was so full of earnestness and sincerity, that soon a large part of the natives had abjured their fetishes, and been baptized as Christians, and a still larger number were wavering on the brink of conversion.

Then the priests, thoroughly alarmed, called a great palaver of the tribe to crush out this threatening evil, before it was too late.

After he had been denounced in many violent speeches, he arose to reply and spoke long and so eloquently that the doubters began to show signs of being convinced. This was too much for one wily old priest, who sprang to his feet, and exclaimed:

"Fine words! Fine words! But what would you do?"

"Do?" answered Anston, "I would die for my faith."

"He has said it! He has said it!" howled the priest, "let him die!"

And the heathens joined in one mighty shout. "Let him die!"

Echoed by most of the waverers, stirred in their savage natures by their thirst for blood, while the converts were cowed into silence.

"I am ready!" said Anston, "I give my life for my faith."

And the priests led him off in triumph to the strong hut which was to be his prison until high noon the next day when he was to die.

As he sat through the long night facing death, he thought sadly of his half-instructed converts, who, if they lost him now, would soon fall back into their degrading fetish worship; but, if he could have a few more years to strengthen their faith, he could win over the doubtful, and leave the whole tribe established Christians.

Had he any right to sacrifice their interest to these quixotic promptings of his conscience? And after all, was it conscience that drove him to his death, and not a morbid desire for heroism and glory even among these savages?

As these thoughts poured through his mind, his fingers closed on the gold point in his pocket. He drew it out, and impressed his commands upon it, when at once it sprang from his hand, and, passing out of the hut began travelling to and fro across the wall, cutting sheer through the palm trunks, of which it was made. One waving bright line after another appeared side by side, as the moonlight shone through the cuts made by the point; and, when this work was done, passing into the hut once more it poured forth a blast like a hurricane, before which the injured wall flew to splinters, leaving a door open to life and freedom.

Then the memory of the moth fell upon him, and he looked out timidly, certain that he should find a gigantic moth blocking his path, but there was none.

The intense tropical moonlight made the whole landscape bright as day, silvered the huts of the kraal, and shimmered on the lake. There was no moth, or insect of any sort to be seen. The path to safety was open.

But was it open? There was no moth, but the thought of it reminded him of the many times he had been misled in the past, and then he saw with startling clearness how great a part the longing for life had played in all his arguments, and that he was deserting his trust.

He sprang through the opening, ran down to the lake and threw the point as far as he could into its gleaming waters. Then he went back to the hut, and sat down to await the end.

Toward morning he heard the pattering of naked feet and a muffled whispering outside the hut and then an exclamation:

"He has gone! He has run away!"

But he called from within,

"No! My children! I am here."

And several of his converts appeared at the opening, and were joined by more, until, when daylight dawned, all the Christians were there squatting in a wide ring about the gap in the wall, hanging on his lips, as he used these last precious hours in strengthening their faith, but still more in trying to instil into them the spirit of Christ; and when at last the priests came to lead him to his death he followed them with the certainty that all his own would be faithful, and with this leaven planted in the tribe he could not for an instant doubt the final result.

He was led to the open space in the middle of the kraal, where the whole tribe was gathered around a tall black, who grasped his savage battle-axe fiercely, waiting for his victim.

Calmly he took his stand beside the executioner in the blinding glare of the tropic sun, when a shadow fell upon him, and, looking up he saw the moth once more, but its wings spread from side to side of the heavens, and gleamed and glowed with all the colors of the rainbow, and at last he knew his guardian angel waiting to take him to Paradise.

An Uncomfortable Night

The talk turned on the haunted house one evening at the club a year ago last spring, which was not surprising, as at that time all talk came around to it in a few minutes, no matter where else it may have started.

I had taken the trouble to look it up, as I suppose almost every one else had, and was disappointed to find it entirely unlike what a haunted house should be. It was a plain brick building as commonplace and respectable as any of its neighbors on that quiet street in the best part of the town; and did not show even a trace of the neglect and decay I had expected, but was conspicuously clean and well kept. As I have said, it was thoroughly commonplace. The only picturesque thing about it was that Madam Ecks had lived there during her meteoric career in our town.

Although I had tried hard to find some definite stories about it, I had not found a single one, so when it came up at the club, I thought:

"Here at last is my chance to get at the facts."

But far from it. Billy Ringore was the only one to shed light upon it, when he burst out with:

"Well anyway! The ghost can't be Madam Ecks. Can any of you fellows think of her as a ghost?"

We all grinned at the idea. It was really too absurd; but this was all. Not one of them could give me a single fact, and yet every man Jack of them believed the house was haunted, and I could not knock the idea out of their solid heads, though I did my best; even when I pointed out that there was not the slightest foundation for their belief, these precious believers could only say feebly:

"That is just what we can't understand. Why can nobody find out how it is haunted?"

"Hna!" said I, "for the very good reason that there are no such things as ghosts, and never have been; and there isn't a soul around here with imagination enough to make up a story about it."

This brought them all down on me and the discussion grew hot, until Tom Nelton said to me:

"For all your talk, I bet you don't dare to pass a whole night in that house."

"What will you bet?" said I.

"A dinner for all this crowd," said he.

This naturally was received with great enthusiasm by the other fellows, and, when I said "Done!" they gave me a round of applause.

"But," said I, "how are we going to manage it? You don't expect me to break into the infernal hole, as well as pass the night in it, do you?"

I hoped this would pull me out of the mess I had got into, but to my disgust Eliott Coltman, who was sitting in a corner apparently buried in his newspaper, looked up with a grin and said:

"I shall be delighted to let you have the keys. I am the agent for the house, but in that case you have got to count me in on the dinner."

So there was no escape for me.

Now that we had a chance to hear the truth at first hand, we overwhelmed Eliott with questions, but with no result. The house had been put in his hands by the heirs of Madam Ecks after her death four years ago; and at first there had been tenants to burn, although none of them ever stayed more than a month at the best; but, as the house began to get a bad name, it grew almost impossible to find any one to live in it.

"It stood empty," said he, "for a year, until a tenant turned up three weeks ago, and he—curse him—left this very morning."

"But what drove him out?" we asked; "that is what we want to know."

"I wish I could find out," said he. "He told me he would not pass another night in that house for anything in the world and, when I asked him what the trouble was, dodged the question as all the other tenants had done. All I could make out was that he had been bothered by a lot of things, which in themselves amounted to little, but grew too much to be borne, when you had to stand them night after night."

"You will be glad to hear," he added, turning to me, "that all the tenants have talked as if the ghost was mischievous, rather than malicious."

Before we went home, it was agreed we should dine at the club the next night, and after dinner the whole crowd would kindly (?) go to see fair play, when I took possession of the haunted house for my twelve hours, beginning at half-past eight that evening.

All the way home I cursed myself for an ass. Why had I got myself into such a hole? It meant an uncomfortable night, even if nothing worse; and now that there was no one to contradict me I did not feel so certain there were no ghosts, but it was too late to back out, and I must show myself a good sport.

As the house had belonged to Madam Ecks, so unpleasantly conspicuous a few years ago, I passed what was left of the evening in raking my memory for everything I knew about her. She came to town from the West before my time, and immediately started to fight her way into good society.

I remembered vividly at one of my first parties seeing a strikingly handsome woman hanging on the lips of the man, with whom she was talking, and knew it must be Madam Ecks, even before I asked. Although little above the middle height, she was cast in such a generous mould that she seemed much taller, and my first thought was:

"What a handsome woman!"

My second "But is not she too handsome? Such voluptuous overflowing beauty is almost too much of a good thing."

Her dress in the extreme of fashion showed and set off her charms to the greatest advantage. It was striking—gorgeous, but again a little too much so. Altogether she seemed to me not quite in good taste; and I felt this even more strongly, when, later in the evening, I happened to pass near her, and breathed in the heavy sensuous perfume, with which she filled the air.

Perhaps I was not quite fair to her, as her affectation in calling herself Madam, instead of Mrs. Ecks, had given me a prejudice against her. She claimed French blood, I believe, and perhaps there was some of it in her veins, but certainly her blonde redundant beauty showed no sign of it. Yet I had to admit she was wonderfully good looking, and, as she knew how to make each man think he was the first and only man for her, it was no wonder that she carried most of them off their feet. For my part I had no chance to try her fascinations, as even then her affair with Senator — was well under way,

She used dinner parties as the principal weapon in her assault upon society; and, as she had a very remarkable cook, and always captured for them some entertaining people, with now and then even a celebrity, they were very attractive, and she made rapid progress; but she did it all so openly, with such a complete want of reserve, that she made herself very ridiculous, and every one laughed at her—those whom she was trying to please with good-natured contempt, while the rungs of the social ladder, which she had cynically left behind, sneered at her with the greatest bitterness.

At the time I saw her she had nearly won the battle, and was trying to make her position entirely secure by marrying Senator —, the great man of our city, who beside coming from one of our best families, was rich and handsome, and had recently made for himself a conspicuous position in the Senate.

It was said he had been an inveterate flirt in his youth, but in spite of that he had never married, and, when Madam Ecks began her pursuit of him in her usual unreserved way, Society enjoyed the sport immensely, and bets were freely made at the club as to whether she would bag him, or not, with the odds very much against her.

But we were wrong, for in due time the engagement came out amid a perfect hubbub of criticism. I got tired of hearing every-where:

"What a pity she caught him! How could he?"

The more, as I could not agree, for to my thinking they were two of a kind. I never had any use for the Senator—a conceited, narrow, self-seeking politician without an atom of statesmanship.

For a month Madam Ecks was in her glory, and then, just on the eve of the wedding, the senator went abroad "for an indefinite stay in Europe," and the whole town burst into roars of laughter at her expense.

"Lost him! Too old a fish to be landed! Served her right!" were the usual comments.

This avalanche of ridicule seemed to crush her, as she disappeared completely from society, and hid her mortification at home.

My Uncle George was the only person I ever heard speak a good word for her. One day when I was making fun of the Madam Ecks engagement, he said:

"Don't talk so, Robert! Poor woman! I am not sure people are right about her. It looks to me more like a case of broken heart than disappointed vanity. At any rate Senator — has behaved like a cad."

I could agree heartily with the last part of his speech, and, although I doubted about the broken heart, Uncle George's opinion made a deep impression on me, because I knew that Madam Ecks had shocked his delicate fastidiousness so much that he would not make her acquaintance.

After this little was heard of her. She kept so closely to her house that I was a good deal surprised to meet her in the street one day some years later. I found her much changed. She had lost a great deal of her beauty, and there was a look of settled depression in her face, which recalled Uncle George's theory of a broken heart; but on the other hand she was beginning to grow fat, and her expression seemed to me lackadaisical and sentimental rather than pathetic. Could not the woman ever be simple and genuine?

She lingered on at least eight years in her retirement, and, when at last she died, had dropped out of sight so completely that she would have been forgotten at once, if the curious stories about her house had not made her again the talk of the town.

The next evening we met at the club, as we had agreed, and after dinner, where they drank the health of "the heroic adventurer," the whole gang sallied out to install me in the haunted house.

We began by looking over the house thoroughly, as should always be done in such cases, and the men made very merry over it, pretending to discover ghosts in all the dark corners. I knew they were doing this to rattle me, but I flatter myself I am above being frightened by that sort of thing, and I was not affected by their fooling in the least, or anyway not enough to speak of.

Finally they gave me a lot of cigars to help me pass the evening, and Billy Ringore even offered me his flask, but that I declined, as, if I was to meet any spirits, I did not want to have it supposed they had come out of a bottle.

Then they bade me good night in their best burlesque vein, one embracing me, and sobbing out on my shoulder:

"Farewell, my brave, my heroic friend!"

Another patting me on the back and saying:

"The nasty ghosty-posties shan't scare dear little Robbie, so they shan't!"

All of which may have been very funny, but I did not feel in the mood for it, so I was well pleased, when I bolted the front door after the last of them.

As soon as I was alone, I began my real examination of the house from cellar to roof; and, after seeing that the back door was bolted, all the windows fastened, and no one hidden anywhere in the lowest story, I looked over the street floor with the same care. The greater part of this was taken up by a large dining-room finished in dark oak with a red wall paper. The heavy chairs were also of oak and covered with red leather, but the two reds did not match, and both were so much too vivid that the effect was gaudy, instead of rich.

Two parlors filled the floor above. They were gorgeously furnished with a perfect swarm of chairs, little sofas, easy-chairs, ottomans, tables and so on. The wooden parts were heavily gilded, wherever they peered out under the swelling masses of upholstery, and these were covered with satin, some of which was violet, and some brilliant red in the front room; while in the back there were three colors, sky-blue, pea-green, and a pink cerise, all of them too bright to go well together; and in the entry between the two a large divan was covered and valanced with glowing golden-orange.

As my taste in colors is more than usually delicate, these rooms set my teeth on edge, but at the same time they did me a great deal of good. Although I am much less easily thrown off my balance than most men, I must confess the monkey tricks of the fellows had shaken me a bit, which was not surprising, as the thought of what might be before me made my nerves decidedly less steady than usual. Now the sight of these rooms at once put me back on my feet again, as it was impossible to think of ghosts or anything not of this earth among such worldly and flamboyant surroundings.

In the next story was Madam Ecks's bedroom furnished with the same oppressively sensuous luxury as the parlors, and like them, haunted by the faint remains of that heavy perfume, which brought back to my mind the party, where I saw her years ago. Time had deadened it, so that it was less overpowering, but had given it a suggestion of decay and death even more repellent than before, if that were possible.

At the back was a spare bedroom, and here the simpler furniture seemed like a breath of fresh air after all that stuffy upholstery. In this room the bed had been made for me with the sheets I had sent to Eliott in the morning.

After I had examined the whole house carefully, and made sure there were no practical jokers hidden in it, and no way for any to get in, I turned on the electric lights all over the place, as later it might be of the first importance to be able to see distinctly, and took the shades off the lamps in the entry between the two rooms, and also from some of them in the front parlor, where I meant to sit, so as to make the light less mysterious than the roseate dusk, which, in the back parlor, filtered as best it could through the thick embroidered pink coverings with which all the lights were shrouded.

Then, as it was only nine o'clock, I established myself in the most comfortable of the many easy chairs, spread out my cigars on one of the gilded tables at my elbow, and opened my novel, for I had realized the danger of imagining horrors, while I was waiting to go to bed, and so had fortified myself against it by bringing with me "The False Faces," said to be the most exciting book of the year, and besides, I had taken the precaution of reading enough of it in the afternoon to get thoroughly interested in the story.

At first my plan worked to a charm, and I became completely engrossed in the thrilling adventures of the Lone Wolf, but before an hour had passed my attention began to wander to my own adventure, and the waiting grew hard to bear. If something was going to happen, why in Heaven's name didn't it begin?

This would not do. So I cast my eyes around on the riot of upholstery, in which I was sitting, and found it a complete antidote for my nervousness, for at once it brought me solidly back to earth. I lighted a fresh cigar, took up my book again, and this time became so wrapped up in it that I lost all sense of my surroundings.

Then a long deep passionate sigh fell upon my ears.

I dropped my book, and with an uncomfortable rising about the roots of my hair, looked over at the corner from which the sound had come, but could see nothing there, and, although I examined that part of the room with the greatest care, found nothing to explain that sigh.

After this it was not easy to fix my attention on my book, but I remembered how effectively my nerves had been calmed twice before by that outrageously frivolous furniture, and so this time I made a complete mental catalogue of it with the happiest result, for after that I was certain I had imagined that sigh, and, if there were ghosts anywhere, I knew there could be none here.

Some little time passed after I had become deep in my book once more and then I was brought up with a start by the rattling of the bead portière—a commonplace sound enough! but what the devil was rattling it in this empty house?

I looked across at it, and there! An arm was drawing it aside. An arm—but where was the body? Through the strings of beads I could see the whole bright entry distinctly, and there was nothing there! Nobody at all! Only an arm! Nothing more!

I *was* frightened. I could only sit, and glare at it, as it slowly drew the clashing portière quite to the door post, and passed out of sight behind it.

For what fearful drama was it drawing the curtain?

It was some minutes before my desperate struggles brought me courage enough to go and look for it, and I succeeded in pulling myself out of my chair and dragging my unwilling feet across to the entry by the sheer force of my will. I had not expected to find anything in that corner behind the doorpost, and yet the shock was none the less dreadful for that, when I found myself confronted by nothing but the solid wall—solid and impassible wood, even if it was painted a delicate rose, panelled with pale blue.

I staggered back to my chair thoroughly unmanned, and sat there trying to brace myself for whatever might come next. What would it be? And, as the time dragged slowly on, and nothing happened—why didn't it come? Anything would be better than this waiting. Would it never end?

But I soon realized that this sort of thing was sapping my nerve and courage, and that I should need all I possessed of both to carry me through what lay before me, so after a stiff fight I managed to pull myself together, lit another cigar, and did the best I could to bury myself in "The False Faces." In this I succeeded, even better than I hoped, as I must have given nearly half my attention to it, although the questions—What will it be? When will it come?—were continually trying to force themselves upon me, and could be kept at bay only by the most desperate efforts.

An hour must have passed in this way, and my struggles with my nerves had got them under fairly good control, when they were set jangling again by a noise from the corner of the room behind me. As before, it was a very common sound—only a chair grating over the floor, as it was moved. But how fearful it was!

I twisted myself around in my chair, and looked into that corner, and, as there was nothing to be seen, I tried to persuade myself I had imagined the noise, but without much success.

Then after a few long minutes it came once more—the grating of a chair dragged across the floor. I sprang to my feet, and turned toward the sound, but all was quiet. Nothing had changed in that corner—yet wait! Was that chair at first so far from the wall? I drove myself to go over and see, but had taken only a few steps, when another noise brought me up standing. It came from the opposite corner, now behind my back, and was the castors of an easy-chair creaking as it moved, and one of them squeaked. I ran across to the chair, pushed it, and it moved with the same creaking of its castors, and one of them squeaked.

My mind was still reeling from this blow, when the swish of satin skirts trailing over the floor came from the entry, and looking out there I saw that the bright yellow divan, though now absolutely quiet, seemed to have moved a few inches away from the wall, but before I could reach it to make certain, I heard for the third time the grating legs of the first chair, and turned quickly enough to catch it moving.

That pale violet satin chair was hitching its gold legs across the floor toward the middle of the room!

This was too much! I dropped into my armchair, as I was no longer able to keep my feet.

Now that I had actually seen one of the chairs moving, the others threw off all restraint, and began closing in on me, the armchairs wheeling toward me on their creaking castors, the other larger ones hitching across the floor with that grating noise, which had grown so hateful to me, while the smaller chairs trotted up, their legs rattling on the polished floor. Behind them came the huge divan trailing its satin skirts and wheezing asthmatically in every joint, and still further in the rear trooped the furniture from the back parlor. Each of them was fighting to be the first to reach me, even the old divan was doing its wheezy best.

As they closed in on me, I thought with a shudder: "What is going to happen, when they reach me? Will they combine to crush me?"

I was not kept long in doubt, for soon the brisk little chairs did reach me, but they paused a few feet away as if overcome by bashfulness, until the two larger chairs, which had been the first to move came up, and shouldering the little fellows aside pressed close to me pushing themselves against my knees; and then all the others thronged up too, struggling and pushing and jostling to get at me. And it was these chairs, whose frivolous worldliness had twice before driven away my terrors, which had now themselves become the most ghastly of them all. Perhaps though not the most ghastly, as this direct attack, which could be seen and felt, was a little less dreadful than the vague threatenings from which I had suffered earlier in the night.

But was not the worst still to come? For all this time I was conscious of some strong emotion animating them. The air seemed to pulsate with it. It lapped me around with horror—a penetrating horror!

What could it be?

I puzzled over it in vain, until suddenly there came to me a shocking enlightenment.

The armchair, in which I was sitting, all at once seemed to grow softer and more yielding. Its arms began to cling about me with a tender pressure, and, although I tried hard not to believe it, there was no question the thing was actually embracing me!

Then the truth burst upon me, and crushed me. They were all pressing on me with affection. No! worse still, with passionate love. So Uncle George had been right! They were pouring out on me all the passionate love, the disappointed longing, which for eight slow years had run to waste in this house, and it was dead, as dead as the ghost of Madam Ecks's perfume that haunted it, and like that full of a vague flavor of decay.

I cannot tell you how utterly revolting I found this stuffy, close, fuzzy longing. This fusty love stuffed with horsehair. It seemed to smother me, to set all my feelings on edge, as when a rough finger is drawn across frayed satin; and the worst of all was my chair with its upholstered endearments.

I could stand them no longer and springing up forced my way through the swarm, which hemmed me in on every side, pushing out of my path the chairs, which fawned on me as I touched them, until I reached the door. There the divan blocked the road. I charged it, and, when it did not move, scrambled over it in spite of the soft clinging satiny fondness, with which it tried to hold me back. Pah!

From its back I gained the stairs with a single jump, and as I bolted up them threw a look behind, and saw the whole pack starting after me. This added wings to my feet, and I did not pause until I had reached my bedroom and locked the door.

I tumbled into the nearest chair—a cane-bottomed one with (thank heaven!) none of the stuffing that could be covered with satin, through which the love could reek and ooze. What a relief it was to escape from that atmosphere of woolly love to air pure enough to breathe freely.

I was only just in time, for I heard the chairs come clattering up from below, their legs rattling on the bannisters, as one jostled another in its eagerness to reach me. Then with a loud crash they threw themselves against the door. How glad I was I had locked it! Let them beat and batter against it as much as they pleased, they could never break it in!

Next I heard that squeaking castor, and knew the armchairs were slowly toiling up from the parlor; and in a minute or two they forced their way through the lighter furniture, shouldering it aside, and the rattling attack on the door gave place to a slow, soft, powerful pressure.

Then I began to feel uneasy. Would the door hold? Were its lower panels bulging already, or did I only imagine they were? How long could they stand it? And how much more terrible than that noisy earlier assault was this steady, slow pressure silent, except when broken by the low creaking of a castor, or once by that detestable squeak!

It seemed as if I sat there for hours watching this stealthy noiseless attack with a desperate certainty that it must succeed in the end. But no! Just as I felt I could bear it no longer, I heard a sudden pushing back of chairs in the entry, and then—welcome sound— the rattling of chair legs against the bannisters, followed by the duller blows from the wadded armchairs, and the nerve-racking squeak of that dreadful castor, all growing fainter and fainter, until all noise died away in the parlor, if I could judge by my ear.

What a long breath of relief I drew, as I realized the attack was over for the time at least! I sank back in my chair pretty nearly used up; and it was many minutes before I grew calm enough even to look at my watch. At first I thought it must have stopped, but no it was going, and I found with a shock that the attack, which seemed to have lasted hours, could not have taken more than twenty minutes.

This was no pleasant discovery, since it meant there were still seven hours, before I was free to go home at half-past eight in the morning. How could I hope to get through them, when only twenty minutes had seemed endless? I thought at first of going to bed, as the time might pass more quickly there, but decided not to, as I felt it was safer to be dressed for the next emergency.

The quiet and freedom from attack, which I had found soothing at first, grew very trying before long, and this anxious waiting for what would come next was much harder to bear than it had been, because in the hurry of my flight I had left my book and cigars in the parlor. When I tried to find some other way of making the time pass more quickly, my brain seemed paralyzed, and in the end I had to put up with counting, as I could think of nothing else.

This did not work half badly, although it was all I could do to keep my mind fixed on it, but at last my determination not to let the waiting affect me, helped by the monotony of the counting bore fruit, and I actually began to feel drowsy.

Then, just as I was dropping off, there came a knock at the door!

A very gentle knock, but it shook me broad awake in an instant,—and in that instant I made up my mind that nothing on earth should make me open the door. So I sat staring at it for a long time; and, as nothing happened, I remembered presently that I had been half asleep, when I thought I heard the knock, and perhaps I had only dreamed it; and then—it came again. This time a number of brisk raps, which gradually became fainter and more timid, as if the courage of the thing in the entry was oozing out, until in the end the noise died into silence.

After this came another pause—a short one—followed by a gentle rap, so modest that I barely heard it, but soon as the thing gained courage the knocks grew louder, until they ended in a furious tattoo, all of a sudden dropping into impressive silence—broken in less than a minute by a succession of knocks, in which, as before, impatience struggled with shyness and timidity.

What was it knocking? It could not be a chair, as these were neither the sharp raps of wood upon wood, nor the gentle blows from a stuffed arm. They came from a knuckle; but whose knuckle? Whose? I must find out! It could not bear to sit there without knowing; and yet the terror of opening that door! What might not be behind it? So I hesitated—not that I was weighing reasons,—I was long past anything of that sort, but while one terror drove me to the door, the other forced me away from it.

As time went on, the suspense grew worse and worse, until it swallowed up completely the dread of what I might find outside; and I ran to the door, turned the key, opened it the merest crack and peered out. One glance was enough and I slammed it back.

Too late! A heavily-gilded chair leg was already thrust between it and the doorpost. I could not shut it, and with a great rush that drove me back, and nearly sent the door flying from its hinges, the furniture burst through and poured swarming into the room.

I slumped into my chair weak with fright, and half smothered by the fusty woolen smell, which loaded the air, and oppressed my lungs like a great featherbed.

The first of the chairs as they surged in, deluged me with their fulsome love, cuddling and caressing my knees, and the wild mass behind jostled, and fought to get nearer to me, and fresh hordes were continually forcing their way into the room.

There were the chairs from both parlors, foremost among them my old enemy with the squeaking castor, and scattered through the mob were the soft clinging, heavily-wadded easy chairs from Madam Ecks's bedroom. I shuddered at the idea of having one of them even touch me. Meanwhile I could hear the old divan at the foot of the stairs wheezing, because she was too big to get up, and from the lower flight came the heavy tramp of the chairs from the dining-room.

But I had no time to shudder at what was coming, for my hands were more than full warding off the exuberant affection of the chairs in front of me, and bad as this was, worse followed, when the later comers closed in on me from behind. What might not happen there, when I could not see them?

And then—and then I felt an eager, hot breath panting against the back of my neck!

This was too much! I sprang from my chair, burst through the crowding furniture, pushing and kicking it to right and left, and reached the top of the stairs. Here I met the heavy dining-room chairs working their way up. The first advanced on me with open arms and an overpowering acrid smell of leather, but with a vigorous kick I sent it flying down the stairs, carrying the others before it, until with a crash they lit in a heap on the divan at the bottom.

I ran down after them, but, when I got to the wreck, it was waiting for me with such fervid spaniel-like longing that I dared not come near it. So getting over the bannisters I clambered down outside them, avoiding all the furniture, except the divan, which managed to stroke my hand as it was clinging to the rail. Urr!

After I had passed the wreck, I leaped back into the entry, ran down the lower flight, and threw myself against the front door. I drew the bolt, pulled back the spring lock, and, as I tore it open, was greeted by a rush of fresh, cool air;—but the door opened only a few inches, because I had forgotten to undo the chain, which I had put up when I locked it.

It was terrible to shut out that breath of freedom, when I had to shut the door to take off the chain, and my fingers trembled, so that for some time I could not draw it from its socket. The appearance of some of the armchairs, which had freed themselves from the wreck, and were hurrying down after me, did not make my nerves the steadier, but at last I succeeded, and threw the door wide open—not a minute too soon, as the leading chair was upon me.

What a relief it was to slam it behind me, and hear the click of its spring lock! And yet in spite of that I ran nearly half a mile before I pulled up thoroughly winded. Then, as I leant panting against a fence, I realized that I was out in the street without my hat or overcoat, but what of that so long as I was out of that house!

I made the best of my way home, but did not feel really safe until I had locked myself into my own house, when at last I re-membered that I had lost my bet. I cared little for that, but it was not pleasant to look forward to the jeers of the other fellows, and nothing could be more disgusting than having to confess myself thoroughly beaten. Yes! There was one thing that was worse—one thing, that I could not face, and that was going back to that house and finishing that uncomfortable night.

Mr. Smith
A Story in the Manner of Hoffmann

Some twenty-five years hereafter Dr. Browne, a young physician, was trying to establish a practice in Boston, and, as he had been altogether too busy to see anything of society in the years before his graduation from the Harvard Medical School, and afterward his dispensary work had left him essentially no time for parties, he began to realize that he had dropped out of sight almost entirely, and that it was of the first importance for him to regain his former acquaintances, if indeed it was not too late even now.

Accordingly he came out of his shell enough to go to a large reception, and, after wandering forlornly about the rooms for an hour or so, drew a friend into a corner, from which they could watch the stream of people flowing by, and asked to be told who these people were, as he could remember but few of them and these only vaguely.

After a few minutes he was most unpleasantly impressed by a man, who was working his way against the stream, and yet there was nothing very unusual about him. He was taller than most people with large staring eyes, a nose hooked like the beak of a parrot, and a dome-shaped head, which, although it rose to a great height above his eyes, gave no impression of intellectual power. It was covered with a sleek thatch of rather long greenish brown hair, and his complexion was a sallow brown of much the same color, but all this was not enough to explain the feeling, which made Dr. Browne shrink from the man as from some slimy animal.

"Who is that?" said he; "the tall man with the slicked-down hair?"

"That?" answered his friend, "oh, that is Jones. Of course, you know Jones. No? Well! Some men like him well enough, but I never had any use for him."

"But who is he?" asked Dr. Browne.

"Who is he? Why everybody knows him. He is—. Well! That's odd! I thought I could tell you all about him, but, when I come to think of it, I don't know who he is. He turned up in Boston a few years ago, and you meet him everywhere."

But Dr. Browne was not listening, for his eye had been caught by two people slowly moving toward them with the crowd. The man's vigorous carriage and hale sturdy appearance was in strange contrast to his crown of snow white hair. It was hard to tell his age. He was certainly far from young, and yet he was so overflowing with energy and power that you felt sure the greatest achievement of his life was still before him. It might be a great poem, a picture perhaps, a symphony, or some other great work in one of the dignified regions of art, but, whatever it was, there could be no question that it would be something of worldwide importance.

He was in ordinary evening dress except—and it was a bizarre exception—that his necktie was sage green instead of white.

The girl by his side was evidently his daughter, but, as descriptions of heroines are always tedious, I will merely ask my readers to recall all the charms of all the heroines of whom they have ever read, roll them into one, multiply them by ten, and then they will have some conception of the attractions of this radiant young person. It is no wonder, therefore, that Dr. Browne was bowled completely off his feet, and seizing his friend's arm asked,

"Who—who is that?"

"Those? Why those are the Smiths," said his friend. "Delightful people! You must know them."

"Smith? Smith?" said Dr. Browne, "the name sounds familiar, but I don't place it."

At this his friend grew somewhat impatient. "Not know them! That is absurd. Of course you know them."

"But who are they?" persisted Dr. Browne.

"Why!" said his friend, "they belong to one of the best families"—and then he stopped evidently puzzled; "but somehow I can't remember any of their relations. All I can say is that since I first met them, it must be three years ago, they have become about the most popular people in Boston, and no wonder for—hullo! What's the matter?"

There was reason for this exclamation, since Jones, who, as I have said, was moving against the stream of people, had by this time come face to face with the Smiths, when the old gentleman, his features distorted with the greatest rage and terror clutched wildly at his collar, as if he were choking, and fell to the ground in some sort of a fit. Jones, after glancing at him with an unpleasant smile, vanished in the crowd; but even sooner Dr. Browne was kneeling by Mr. Smith and treated his fainting-fit, or whatever it was, with so much skill and energy that in a few minutes his patient was able to walk into another room, where he lay on a sofa, until a car could be brought to take him home.

Dr. Browne, as he helped him into it, asked if he might call the next day to see whether he had suffered from this attack, and was most cordially invited to do so, while Miss Smith turned on him a look of gratitude, which sent him home wondering whether he was not in the seventh heaven, rather than prosaic Boston.

The next morning, long before the proper hour for calling, he was at the address given him by Mr. Smith. It was in an out of the way quarter of the town on the north side of Beacon Hill, built up originally with fine comfortable dwellings, but now sadly faded, and overrun with boarding houses. Here Mr. Smith had established himself in a house which, although far from modern, was full of a quaint old-fashioned charm.

The door was opened by a neat servant girl, who invited Dr. Browne into the "library," while she told her master he had come. This was a room at the back of the house, certainly most inappropriately named, as there were no books. It looked, in fact, much more like a greenhouse than a library, as the whole of the back wall had been taken out, and replaced by a great window, which was flooding the room with sunlight. Pushed close to this glass was a writing table, but even this seemed not to belong to a library, as the only thing on it was a large flower-pot, or perhaps I should call it tub, of beautifully decorated glazed earthenware full of earth, but looking strangely empty with no sign of the magnificent plant, which it ought to have held.

He had hardly taken in these details, when Mr. Smith came downstairs. He was wearing a dressing-gown of sage green—evidently his favorite color—and now in the full light of day Dr. Browne was struck even more than last night with the overflowing vigor and energy of the man, and yet he decided that he was much older than he had thought at first.

Altogether, he found himself wonderfully attracted by this sturdy and benevolent patriarch, who on his side was very glad to see him, and full of thanks for his help the night before.

Just as he had said he was none the worse for his misadventure, Dr. Browne heard the rustle of a dress, and turning greeted Miss Smith with so much effusion that he felt somewhat afraid her father might object, and, glancing at him out of the tail of his eye saw to his intense surprise, in place of an old gentleman in a green dressing-gown, a superb century plant growing in the flower-pot on the table.

But when he whirled around to see this astonishing sight plainly, he found that his eyes had put a strange trick upon him, for there was Mr. Smith standing by the table with a pleasant smile upon his face, and the flower-pot was empty as before.

This first call led to many more, and for some time the course of true love seemed to be running smoothly, in spite of the proverb.

A week or two later Dr. Browne had a very strange dream. He found himself walking through a picturesque old-fashioned street—it might be in this country, or perhaps in Europe—when he was lifted up in the air, so that he could look into a second-story window, and through this he saw a large room, which seemed to be some sort of workshop, or laboratory. Its walls were lined with tables covered with apparatus, some of it chemical, some physical, while other pieces entirely unknown to him were exceedingly complicated and strange, but the occupant of the room was stranger still—

A huge cuttle-fish—an octopus—crawling about on its long tentacles, and collecting a number of things from the different tables, which it carried to the middle of the room, and threw upon a chafing-dish full of glowing coals.

At last it crawled up to a block between two tables, seized a hatchet with the suckers of one of its arms, and putting another on the block chopped off the end of it. Then, after it had thrown this tip on the hot coals, it scuttled out of the room, as fast as it could, slamming the door behind it, and Dr. Browne knew (as one does in dreams) that this door was edged with rubber, and pressed into place by a powerful screw, so as to close absolutely air tight.

Now a pale blue vapor rose from the glowing coals, and Dr. Browne awoke nearly beside himself with terror.

As he came fully to himself, he realized he had been awakened by a loud knocking at his chamber door, and found that it was his landlady with word that a man was very sick in his medical district, and he was needed at once.

After he had dressed as quickly as possible, and hurried to the place, he found the case was indeed a very serious one. The man was desperately sick, and showed violent and alarming symptoms, of which the most striking was the appearance of his tongue, as it was bright sky blue and lolling out of his mouth. The other symptoms, though not so startling as this, were as characteristic from a medical point of view, but—and this was very strange—showed a disease entirely unlike any known to Dr. Browne, either by experience, or reading, so that he had to work entirely in the dark, and his attempt to check its progress led to no result whatever. The best he could do was to try to relieve the sufferings of the victim, and in this he was fairly successful.

In the course of the day he snatched time enough from the bedside of his patient to consult one of the best of the older Boston physicians, who, however, had met with no such case even in his great experience and wide reading, so he could only suggest a few more alleviations for the sufferings of the patient.

The next morning the man died at half past five, exactly twenty-four hours after he had been taken sick, and immediately three new cases of the disease appeared in the next two houses. These, like the first, ran their course, and killed their victims in twenty-four hours, and were followed at once by five new cases, and so it went on. Death invariably followed the attack in twenty-four hours, and then new cases appeared, always two more than on the preceding day.

It seemed almost as if there were only virus enough to poison a certain number of people, and that it was imprisoned so securely in the bodies of these patients that it could seize no new victims, until it had been set free by the death of those already attacked. If this theory were true, it followed that the amount of virus was slowly increasing, enough being formed each day by its growth in the bodies of its victims to infect two more persons.

One of the most remarkable things about the disease was that it attacked the people only directly in front of it, so that, moving neither backwards, nor sideways, it travelled along a single line spreading out like a fan, as more houses were affected by the increase in the number of victims; and its greatest virulence followed the axis of this fan, as shown by the number of cases here, or, in other words, by the number of deaths, for no patient ever recovered.

As soon as the threatening nature of the epidemic was realized, the doctors of Boston hurried to the rescue, and, when on the tenth day one hundred cases had been reported, it ceased to be a local affair, and the health authorities called into consultation the best medical men in the country, but with no result beyond establishing the fact that such a disease had never been heard of before.

Of the many suggestions made for its control the only one that seemed promising was to remove the entire population from the regions on which the disease was advancing, but, before this could be carried out, it was proved useless, as many people had run away from houses threatened by the epidemic, but on the day when it reached these houses the proper number of their inhabitants were stricken, whether they had stayed in its track, or had taken refuge in other parts of the city, or even in distant towns. This stern undeviating regularity with which it seized the victims it had marked down, was one of the most dreadful and strangest of the many strange things about the disease. The cases outside the region of its first attack did not, however, become new centres of infection, as, after the death of the patient, no more cases occurred in that neighborhood.

Dr. Browne worked early and late over the victims, and, as his experience increased, became very successful in reducing their sufferings, although he found nothing to check the inexorable advance of the disease.

On the evening of the eighteenth day, which brought the whole number of deaths to over three hundred, as he crossed Cambridge Street on his way home to his lodgings, suddenly he realized that the deadly axis of the epidemic was aimed straight at the house of Mr. Smith. At first the horror of it struck him motionless, then after a minute of intense thought his eyes flashed with sudden inspiration, and he hurried off to the telegraph office, and sent a message to a scientific friend in Cuba. Two hours later the flying express brought to his lodgings four large earthenware jars from this friend, and, as the expressman was carrying one of them upstairs, he knocked out the bung by accident, and saw to his surprise that it was full of what seemed to be dirty brown slime.

Dr. Browne now locked himself into his room, and stayed there all through the next day, not even coming out for his meals, which were left outside his door by his landlady according to his orders; and the policeman on that beat noticed that his light was burning the whole of the first and second night.

About five o'clock on the second morning his landlady was awakened by a loud noise, and on calling out:

"What was that?"

Dr. Browne's voice answered,

"It was nothing, Mrs. Robinson. My friend tumbled downstairs, that was all! We shall be back to breakfast."

Mrs. Robinson, running to the window, saw him come out arm in arm with a stranger, and at once was devoured with curiosity.

"Who could it be? And how did he get into the house?" For she knew that no one had come to see Dr. Browne. Nothing should prevent her from getting to the bottom of this mystery, when they came back to breakfast.

Meanwhile, at half-past five, Dr. Browne and his friend reached Cambridge Street, just as the disease was springing across it to keep on its terrible course up Beacon Hill. They stopped here for a minute, and Dr. Browne took off a cloak, which his friend wore over his left shoulder, and then quickly put it back again.

From that instant the epidemic vanished! It had gone as mysteriously as it came.

When later Mrs. Robinson brought in their breakfast, although she stared with all her eyes at Dr. Browne's friend, it was no use. She had never seen him before, that was certain, as no one, who had seen him once, could forget him, he was so inconceivably uncouth, rough-hewn, unfinished. His shapeless features were jumbled into his face anyhow, and seemed not more than half-made; his motions were so untrained and clumsy, that she was not surprised he had fallen downstairs. The clothes, in which this unattractive person was dressed, she recognized as a suit of Dr. Browne's, and even at the breakfast table he wore a cloak over his left shoulder.

After a few days had proved that the epidemic had really disappeared, Dr. Browne found time to begin calling on the Smiths once more. These calls, however, were not so pleasant as the earlier ones, because his friend always came with him, and there could hardly have been a more complete spoilsport than this crude formless being, whose mind seemed quite as ill made as his body, for, when Mr. Smith took pity on the uncouth young man, and tried to draw him into the talk, he answered with unintelligible grunts, and Dr. Browne hastened to take up the conversation in his place.

It would certainly have been more pleasant, if Dr. Browne had come alone, but this never happened. His lumpish friend was always at his elbow, and, as the two plainly had nothing in common, his friends began to speculate on the nature of the hold this disagreeable creature had upon him.

Even, when somewhat later Dr. Browne went to a man's dinner, he accepted only on condition he could bring his friend, who came wearing the inevitable cloak over his left shoulder, and was established on his right by Dr. Browne, who found to his great satisfaction that Mr. Smith was sitting on his left. Directly opposite was an empty chair for some guest, who had not yet arrived.

The soup went off, and the chair was still vacant, but, when they were half way through the fish, the missing guest turned up, and proved to be Jones—the decidedly repellent person whom Dr. Browne had seen at a reception some time before. Mr. Smith at once became very much agitated, and sprang to his feet muttering:

"I can't stand that scoundrel!"

But Dr. Browne managed to quiet him enough to avoid a scene, although after he had unwillingly taken his seat again, he could not help throwing furtive glances at Jones, which were full of hatred with an evident dash of fear.

As for Dr. Browne he determined to keep his eyes open and it was well that he did so, for presently, when Mr. Smith was looking the other way, he saw Jones reach across the table, and drop a powder into his glass of water. (Mr. Smith, by the way, drank only water—no wine, or tea, or coffee.) This was hardly done, when Mr. Smith put out his hand for his glass, but, before he could take it, Dr. Browne, by what looked like an accident, knocked it off the table, and broke it.

Later in the dinner, after the water had been wiped up, and the pieces of glass taken away, Dr. Browne happening to put his hand on the napkin in his lap felt something crawling under his fingers, and, looking down, saw a mass of swarming black worms covering that part of his napkin, which had been wet by the water. Ugh!

After dinner, rather against his will, Dr. Browne was introduced to Jones, who shook hands with a clinging grasp distinctly unpleasant, and this distaste gave place to an absolute shudder, when he felt that Jones had lost his little finger.

He got away from Jones as soon as he could, and then Mr. Smith, who was still restless and troubled, suggested to him that they should go for a walk, and, accordingly after excusing themselves to their host, they started on one of the evening tramps, for which Mr. Smith had such an especial taste that they had often wandered together through out-of-the-way parts of the city at strange hours of the night.

On this occasion the three, for Dr. Browne's friend came too, were walking through a dingy street in the lower part of the town, when a second story window was pushed up, and a quantity of ink thrown over Mr. Smith.

"It is that scoundrel, Jones!" he shouted. "He is always playing me some dirty trick."

And, as the window came down, there was an unpleasant chuckle from the man inside. But Dr. Browne did not notice it, for suddenly it came upon him that this was the window through which he had looked in his dream, and it was in the very next house that the epidemic had started.

That night a painful irritation in his right hand made it hard for Dr. Browne to sleep. It was due, he found, to a number of inflamed little blisters oddly arranged in three nearly parallel rows and a fourth at an angle to the others. It was nothing serious, but certainly very strange, and he wondered what could have caused it.

But next morning he had no thoughts for such trifles, as this was to be the fateful day when he meant to put his fortune to the touch. He had asked Miss Smith to see him at noon, and punctually to the minute he was at her house. The parlor maid told him Miss Smith was in her sitting room upstairs, but there was his lumpish friend tied to his elbow as usual. Now, I have always understood that the saying "two is company, but three is a crowd" applies to an offer of marriage more completely than to anything else. At any rate, Dr. Browne thought so, and for once he left his companion behind, as he ran upstairs; but before he had time to get fairly started in what he had come to say, he was interrupted by a tremendous squealing, howling, and yelping from the floor below. He sprang to his feet with a smothered exclamation, which it was as well Miss Smith did not hear, and ran downstairs, and when she hurried after him she found her King Charles spaniel rolling on the floor in great distress with its tongue lolling out of its mouth and bright blue, while Dr. Browne was putting the cloak over the left shoulder of his lumpish friend.

But, before she could ask what it meant, they heard a frightful crash of splintering glass from the library, and Miss Smith gasped:

"My father!"

Dr. Browne rushed to the rescue, and not a moment too soon. In the flower pot on the table stood an immense century-plant, just showing a bud amid its circle of leaves, and through a great hole broken in the glass wall a huge cuttle-fish was crawling, which, as the strangeness of it all held Dr. Browne motionless, made its way up on the table with almost incredible speed, stretched its long tentacles out over the leaves of the century-plant, and brought its great parrot beak around to nip out the bud.

But now Dr. Browne threw himself on the monster with such a volley of blows, that it stopped its attack on the century-plant, until it had got rid of this new enemy.

Its great arms wound themselves around him with a fearful crushing grip. The bell-shaped suckers on their slender stalks dragged and pulled so savagely that they seemed to tear out great pieces of his flesh. Its two huge staring eyes were glaring at him to find new places for an attack, while the parrot beak was slowly working its way round to reach his eyes, and tear them out. But almost worst of all was the prostrating nausea and loathing, which always attacks one in the grasp of a cuttle-fish.

It was an unequal struggle! Dr. Browne tore with all his strength at the arms already wound about him, but he might as well have tried to wrench off part of his own body; and now three more of its feelers were beginning to enfold him in their deadly coils. His right arm was bound fast to his side, and his left, although still free, could not long avoid the writhing tentacles, which were feeling and reaching for it.

This then was the end! But, as he threw a faint despairing look around, his eyes fell on his lumpish friend watching the struggle with a grin of inane amusement on his unshaped features. Summoning the whole of his remaining strength, Dr. Browne with the one hand which was still free, snatched the cloak away from his shoulder. Then a pale blue vapor floated out from the empty coat sleeve, and struck the cuttle-fish an overwhelming blow. A terrific shudder convulsed its huge round body. The horrible suction relaxed. The pressure of the tentacles slackened; it shrank and shrivelled to nearly half its size, and with another spasm, which shook its whole frame, dropped from its victim dead.

What happened to Dr. Browne's lumpish friend was hardly less astonishing, for he suddenly collapsed, leaving nothing but a suit of old clothes lying in a puddle of slime.

After this it was not necessary for Dr. Browne to repeat the question, which had been interrupted so rudely. No more words were needed! Miss Smith caught him as he was falling and supported the victorious, but grievously shaken hero to the sofa, where they sat hand in hand, until both had recovered some degree of calmness.

Then all other feelings were lost in wonder at the miracle of the blossoming century-plant. The great stem shot up its full eight feet in as many minutes, the branches thrust out from its summit teemed with buds, which flew open in glorious bloom; and then these delicate bells began to wave and sway, as if moved by a gentle breeze, and from them flowed a sweet faint music gradually swelling into song.

How I wish I could give you Mr. Smith's paean of triumph as the lovers heard it! But it was repeated to me only once, so I should have to "garble from memory," as Mr. Jabberjee says; and I am sure my halting remembrance would mar the tender harmony and music of the poetry. I must content myself, therefore, with giving only the substance of it in plain prose.

Mr. Smith then, or, as we must call him now, the Prince of the Vegetable Kingdom, described in glowing verse his love for the

mortal whom he made his bride in defiance of the laws of the Kingdom, and for this the king, his father, decreed that he should be
banished to the earth until his time of flowering.

Those first years, made happy by their love and the birth of
their daughter, were far from a punishment, before the death of
his dear wife crushed all this happiness; but even after that, when
time had dulled this pain, the years in Boston brought him content and peace, until his bitterest enemy—a cuttle-fish—discovered
his retreat, and in the guise of Jones pursued him to the earth to
kill him.

After every one of his first attacks had come to nothing, the
cuttle-fish grew desperate enough to let loose on him a frightful
poison, which owed much of its venom to a piece cut from one of
his own tentacles. The slightest whiff of this was instant death to a
cuttle-fish, but it could not kill a Vegetable Prince, until it had
grown into a monstrous plague in the bodies of five hundred human beings.

It was terrible to sit helpless grieving over the fearful destruction of human life, and watching this grim inevitable fate speed-
ing upon him, until that fortunate day when the epidemic vanished
and his life was saved.

After this incredible event had foiled this assault upon his life,
Jones was compelled to wait with sullen patience, till his time of
blossoming, when he could be destroyed by nipping out his bud,
while all his energies absorbed in the travail of flowering left him
no power to ward off the attack.

From this fate he had been saved only by the heroic bravery of
his dear son; but what, he asked, was the strange and mysterious
weapon which killed their monstrous enemy, and Dr. Browne answered:

"When I saw the fatal disease rushing upon my dearest friends,
there flashed into my mind like an inspiration a plan for stopping
it by constructing a man from primeval slime and the amoebiform
protoplasm of the sponge. I left off one of his arms to make an
opening, through which his spongy tissue absorbed the virus, when,

after killing one set of victims, it was springing upon the next; and then I kept the deadly vapor safely in his body by means of a cloak worn over his shoulder, until it was poured forth so opportunely to save us all from the tentacles of the cuttle-fish."

A few days after the flowering of the Century Plant brought his banishment to an end, three very happy people set out for the Vegetable Kingdom; and, although Dr. Browne's professional duties cut short his stay in that delightful region all too soon, it was not more than a month before he left Boston again for his wedding to his dear "Miss Smith," which the Prince celebrated with impressive state.

Since their marriage the young people live in Boston, but, as Dr. Browne has a most efficient associate, they are able to spend a good part of each year in long blissful visits to "Mr. Smith" in the Vegetable Kingdom.

The Cube

Plashkill, like so many other Hudson River towns, dozes peacefully between the river and the creek, from which it takes its name; and there lived in a pleasant old house on the outskirts of the village the girl, who was the victim of this strange experience.

One hot day toward the end of September, now many years ago, she started for a morning's fishing, and after five minutes' walk on the dusty road was glad to turn into the woods beside the creek, where it was cool enough to be pleasant, though still too warm for anything but leisurely sauntering. It was some time, therefore, before she came to the fishing place she liked best, a flat mossy rock jutting out into a more than usually tranquil reach of the stream, and so completely shaded by trees that they almost dipped their branches into the water. Here she established herself comfortably and was soon dreamily watching her float, since even in this shade it was too hot to take a lively interest in anything.

The morning slipped away pleasantly in lazy meditation, now and then perhaps even in dozing, and the fishes seemed to be as languid as she, for not even a nibble disturbed her float.

At length the noon bells from the distant village warned her that dinner time was approaching, and she thought with comical dismay of the shower of chaff which would burst upon her, if she came home empty handed after her boasts at the breakfast table of the number of fish she was going to catch. But, if the fish would not bite, what could she do? All she could think of was to allow herself ten minutes more, when at last it was time to start for home; and, after these had brought nothing, two minutes more for luck.

These passed too, and she was just pulling in her line to go home, when a tremendous bite dragged the float deep under the water, and nearly jerked the pole out of her hands. In an instant she was all alive to land this fish, which must be large enough to make up for bringing home no others. After a short but fierce struggle she managed to pull her hook to the surface, but it flew out of the water with such a bounce that she thought she had lost him; and, indeed, at first the hook seemed empty, but when she looked more carefully, she saw on it what appeared to be a little square of flesh.

It was about half an inch across and certainly could not have pulled so tremendously. This made her examine it with a good deal of curiosity, and she found it was an irregular cube of what looked like raw meat, except on one side, which was covered with an unhealthy yellowish skin; the others were rough with projecting fibres like a piece of tough beef cut with a dull knife; and the worst of it was, the disgusting thing was alive. The fibres were vibrating with a slow waving motion, which seemed to reach out for some prey, and every now and then the whole mass was shaken with a convulsive jerk, as if it were trying to open and shut like some of the larger jelly-fishes.

Altogether it was so inexpressibly loathsome, that she could not bring herself to touch it, but tried to rub it off her hook upon the rock; and, when this failed, pried and pushed at it with a stick; and at last, when she could not get rid of it, utterly overcome with disgust, she threw into the creek hook, line, rod and all, and hurried away from this unclean spot.

After leaving it well behind, she sank down on the pine-needles breathless and thoroughly unstrung; but soon the soft warm air, and the green quiet of the woods soothed her jangled nerves enough for her to start for home; and, before she got out of the woods, she had so far recovered her usual cheerful serenity that she began thinking what a good story she could make out of her adventure.

Just beyond the woods she caught sight of a belated water-lily growing in the creek so near a log, which reached out into the stream, that she could pick it easily; and, as it was an uncommonly fine one, she decided to bring it home with her, as it would at least be something to show for her morning. Accordingly she rolled up her sleeve, and cautiously ventured out to the end of the slippery log. Then to get the longest possible stem she plunged her arm under water nearly to the shoulder, and, just as her fingers closed about the cool smooth stem, she felt on her upper arm a prick like the bite of a leech, and drawing it out quickly there was the cube clinging to it, as a shell-fish sucks itself on to a rock.

It was a mercy that she did not tumble off the log! And only by the use of the utmost self-control could she manage to totter back to the shore. There, although she shrank in every fibre from the loathsome thing, she seized it and tried to wrench it off her arm, but her fiercest struggles did not even stir it. Next she scraped at it feverishly with a sharp piece of slate, but with no success; so that at last she was obliged to pull down her sleeve over it and go home.

During this short hot walk she shuddered at herself, for she could not help feeling disgraced by the presence of this unclean thing upon her arm; and it was a very flushed, unstrung girl who sneaked into the house, and crept up to her room. Here she rolled up her sleeve again, almost hoping to find nothing, as it seemed too horrible to be true, but there it was still clinging to her arm, and it was the very cube she had caught further upstream, for she saw the mark of her hook in its yellow mottled skin.

This time she was bound to get it off, but she pulled, pushed and tore at it in vain, even when she grasped it with a towel to get a firmer hold on its slimy surface; and, when the dinner bell rang, she had to pull her sleeve over it once more, and go down to the table.

There, as her brothers had heard she brought home no fish, the expected chaff broke loose.

"Soup? No thank you!" said one; "I will wait for Daphne's fish."

"It must have been an awfully big haul," said the other. "See how heated she got carrying such a pile home."

"I hope we shan't get perfectly sick of fish, before we get them all eaten up."

Instead of, as usual, meeting this feeble teasing with a lively crushing answer, Daphne, to the dismay of all, burst into tears, and hurried out of the room.

In her chamber she locked the doors, and attacked the cube once more, and when she found again she could not stir it, tried her best to cut it off with a knife but could not make even the slightest impression on its tough surface. Then, thoroughly desperate, she made up her mind to cut out of her arm the piece of flesh, to which it was clinging, but the first cut bled so much that she grew frightened, and dared go no further. In fact, she found it no easy matter to stop the blood.

When at last she succeeded, she had hardly collapsed a limp, hopeless mass of wretchedness on the couch, when her mother came knocking at the door, and asked tenderly what was the matter. It was hard not to throw herself on her lap, and tell her everything, but the loathsome thing stood between them like some secret too shameful to be confessed even to her mother, and all she could do was to sob on her shoulder, and say she was very miserable.

After soothing her as best she could, her mother left her trying to go to sleep, and hoped that the next day would bring Daphne back to her old wholesome self, but it did not. Nor the one after that, nor many days to come.

The shrinking consciousness of her loathsome parasite was always with her, and oppressed her with a sense of disgrace, as if she were guilty of some shameful crime; for, unreasonable as it was, she could not get rid of the feeling that in some way she was to blame. Under this strain her health gave way rapidly. A nervous, anxious look never left her face, and she grew so thin and pale that they feared she was going into a decline. Her appetite, however, instead of falling off, as would have been natural, actually increased, until she was eating enough for two, so that one of her brothers indulged in the time-worn joke that, if she had consumption, it was only consumption of food. The doctor when summoned could find no disease, spoke of a nervous shock, and was plainly puzzled.

As the weeks dragged into months, her health continued to run down, for, instead of getting accustomed to the cube upon her arm, her hatred and disgust for it increased. This terrible repulsion, however, was the only cause of her sufferings, since the cube gave no physical pain, in fact, she would not have known it was there, had it not been for an occasional slight suction on her arm.

Meanwhile, its appearance changed but little. Toward the end of the third month the red parts had grown more purple, and the whole, although its size was unaltered, had taken on a bloated over-fed look, a change, slight as it was, which made it even more repulsive than before, if that were possible.

One day not long before Christmas an errand took her to the village, and, as she reached the bottom of the hill on which her house stood, she felt suddenly a most intense relief, a cheerful buoyancy unknown to her for months. Full of a wild hope she turned into a retired lane that ran along the foot of the hill, and hastening down it, until she was out of sight of the road, rolled up her sleeve and—she was not deceived. The cube was gone!

All the way to the village she walked on air, greeting the acquaintances she met with all her old time vivacity, and started for home briskly, as she was anxious to look at her arm again, and make sure the good news was really true.

On her way home at the foot of the hill she met a girl, whom she did not know, which was strange, as the village was so small that she must have heard, if any guest from out of town was staying in it. This girl, too, looked curiously familiar, although she could not remember where she had seen her before, but this puzzle was driven out of her head by the excitement of reaching home, when she flew to her room, rolled up her sleeve, and it was true; The cube was really gone. It had dropped off, leaving a barely perceptible scar.

She went down to dinner overflowing with the wildest of spirits. To the delight of every one it was the real Daphne again, in place of the silent, dejected wraith of the last three months; and the rest of the day was a little triumphal celebration of her return to herself.

It was later than usual, therefore, when at last she sat before the glass in her room combing out her hair for the night, and happily thinking over the great deliverance of the day.—And then in the glass she saw the door behind her slowly pushed open, and wondered, who could be coming to her room at this time of night. Very slowly it opened wider and wider, until at last a girl dressed in white with a comb in her hand stood in the doorway, peering into the room. It was the stranger, she had met in the morning, and now she saw why it had looked so familiar.

It was herself!

Herself even to the least detail.

Slowly the thing crept toward her, while she, paralyzed with terror, sat watching it in the glass.

Nearer it crept and nearer, until close behind her it crouched to spring at her. Then the spell was broken. Her courage came back in a flood, and springing to her feet she turned, and faced it—and it went. She never could tell how, whether it vanished, or ran from the room, but it went.

This was too much for her over-strained nerves, and running into her sister's room, she said she must sleep with her.

"What is the matter?" said her sister. "Have you seen a ghost?"

"No! (rather doubtfully). But I am frightened, terribly frightened."

Her sister laughed at her for being afraid of nothing, but was quite willing to take her in for the night.

What a relief it was to take refuge under her sister's wing! And when at last she nestled down in bed be side her, she felt entirely safe, although still too excited and shaken to go to sleep for a long time.

In the early dawn she started broad awake in quivering horror, and, as her eyes opened, they met the cruel glare of that hateful thing, which with its face almost touching hers was kneeling on her chest, while its smooth slender fingers felt for her throat. With a wild shriek she grasped her sister's arm, and it went.

After this it was always near her. She soon found that it never ventured to come in, unless she was alone, but, if she was alone even for a minute, in it peered through the window, or slowly the door began to open, and she felt it was there, so she had to make sure that some one was with her all the time. This was hard to manage, but it had to be, as the slightest gap in her watchfulness showed her the double close at hand lying in wait for her.

Although constant vigilance saved her from an actual clash with her follower, she found this so trying that often she was tempted to meet it face to face, and dare it to do its worst, but each time the mysterious uncanny horror which enveloped it was too much for her courage.

At first the nights were times of terror, but a long and wearing trial at last proved to her that sleeping with her sister was a complete protection, in spite of her horrible experience the first night.

Even with quiet nights, however, this last state was much worse than the three months, when she was nourishing the cube upon her arm. Then shame and disgust were all she had to endure. Now it was a gnawing suspense and an always threatening danger. Her anxious worried expression became very painful, her nerves were completely out of tune, and she grew even more thin and pale.

Her mother, thoroughly alarmed, was at her wits' end to find some way to help her, and, when early in the winter Plashkill was excited by the prospect of a party, urged Daphne to go, hoping that the change might do her good. At first she would not hear of it; but on thinking it over she realized that, as the cube appeared only when she was alone, a crowded party would be the safest place possible, and so agreed to go and even looked forward to it with a good deal of pleasure.

When the evening came she enjoyed herself so thoroughly that she almost forgot her hated double. For one thing, she was dancing the German with John, which was happiness enough, and beside, as she was very popular, she was taken out much of the time.

In one of the figures, which resembled a quadrille, she started forward in ladies' chain looking back over her shoulder to throw some lively remark at her partner, when, as her hand met that of the other girl, she felt those long smooth, slender fingers, which had once fumbled for her throat, and looking around met the mocking gaze of the Thing. She was actually hand in hand with it! With a convulsive shudder she tried to tear her hand away from those dreadful fingers, but they clung like a shellfish to its rock; and, when at last they reluctantly drew themselves off, they left her so shaken that she could hardly force herself to keep on dancing.

On her return, when she passed the Thing once more, she took the best of care to keep her hand well out of its reach, for she could not have borne its touch a second time.

As she got back to her place, she began to wonder how the Cube had found a partner, and looking across saw it was dancing with Eben Trissell, the most able and successful young man in the village, and so attractive and lively that even his goodness was forgiven. Evidently, too, this was no chance meeting, for they were chatting and laughing together with the intimacy of an old friendship. Then she saw the Cube draw his attention to her, and both looked at her with a strange hungry eagerness, which was really terrible.

All this time Daphne had been holding herself up only by sheer force of will. She kept saying to herself: "I won't give way! I won't! I won't!"

And for a few minutes more she managed to totter through her part of the dance, but then it became too much for her, and she grew so faint, that she had to ask her partner to take her back to her seat.

This broke up the set. The music stopped, and her friends crowded around her full of sympathy and clumsy attempts to help her. Foremost among them was the Cube, and it was actually offering to stroke her forehead. This was too much! She could not have endured the touch of those loathsome fingers with their veiled suggestion of slimy horrors, and staggering to her feet asked to be taken home at once. John was more than ready to escort her, and, after she had refused to drag her sister from the half-finished party, they were soon on their way.

The sharp, crisp air and the winter moonlight lying on the fresh snow quieted her nerves, and presently she began to wonder what the Cube had looked like to other people, and so asked John:

"Who was it dancing with Eben Trissell?"

John began to answer—then stopped puzzled, and after a little hesitation said:

"Bless me, if I know! It is queer too, as I thought I noticed especially, but now I can only remember it was a pretty girl."

Daphne smiled at the unconscious compliment, but was not surprised at the vagueness of John's impression of the Cube; and, when in the next few days she took occasion to ask several of the girls the same question, all of them either had forgotten who danced with Eben Trissell, or, if they named his partner, it was a girl who had danced with some one else.

After this no more parties, as, instead of proving the safest of places, this one had exposed her to the Cube so cruelly.

The winter dragged its slow length wearily along, and her health sank lower and lower under the incessant strain, with her enemy always just out of sight on the watch to pounce on her; until, as February drew to an end, her condition grew so alarming that her mother bitterly regretted her inability to send her to a warmer climate, and could only hope for an improvement when Spring had fairly come at last.

Daphne, by constant brooding on this murderous persecution, gradually came to understand that the Cube, while clinging to her arm, had absorbed enough of her nature to take on her bodily appearance and perhaps even her character, and now it was lying in wait to kill her, so that by appropriating her soul it could take her place in the world, condemning her to utter extinction. The thought of this loathsome thing taking her place with her mother, or with John stiffened her weakening courage, and she vowed, if she must succumb, it should be only after fighting to the last fibre of her strength and endurance.

One bright day late in March, John came to invite her to go with him and see the breaking-up of the ice, which was being driven out of the creek by a heavy freshet. She accepted this attractive invitation gladly, because there was not the least chance that John would leave her alone.

The day was sunny, and, although blustering—as March should be—very pleasant, especially as the sun and wind of the morning had dried the ground, making excellent walking, in spite of the heavy rains of the last two days.

After a brisk walk of a mile and a half they reached an ideal place for seeing the flood, for here a low but precipitous hill jutted out into the stream, which swept in a wide curve around its base, brawling through a narrow valley, that might fairly be called a gorge.

They stood here for some time, watching the cakes of ice sailing down the stream above, until reaching the narrow throat of the gorge they were jostled, and thrown together, grinding against, or over each other, and piling up on the farther shore of the bend, or elbowing their way past, and then fighting savagely for a passage through the constantly narrowing channel. It was a most thrilling sight, more like a battle of fierce barbarians, than the crash of inanimate ice.

The flood evidently had been very bad farther up the creek, as now and then fence-rails, uprooted bushes, or even trees were whirled down amid the ice, and the rush of this great mass of water between the cramping banks would alone have been well worth seeing without the savage grinding and crashing of the great blocks of ice.

As they were watching this wonderful sight, they saw far up the stream something dark lying on one of the ice-cakes. The level rays of the sun were so dazzling that for some time they could not make out what it was; but, as it came nearer, there was even through the glare a suggestiveness about its shape that sent the blood from their cheeks.

Nearer it came and nearer, until at last they could see clearly that their worst anticipations were too true. It was a woman lying on her face apparently collapsed by terror. Daphne seized John's arm convulsively.

"Do something! We must do something!"

And John, whose mind had worked quickly, shouting, "I may catch her lower down!" started down the hill at the top of his speed, barely hearing Daphne's agonized cry of, "Go! Do go!"

It was the only chance of rescuing the poor woman, for by running across the hill John could strike the creek where it spread into the broader channel, before the cake of ice had time to get through the longer winding gorge; and in this quieter water there was a chance he might reach and save her, which it would have been madness to attempt amid the turmoil of the gorge.

If only there would be ice enough left to float her but, even before it had entered the gorge, great pieces had been broken from the cake, and Daphne shuddered, as she thought of it mauled and crushed by the frightful blows of the jostling cakes.

As she was straining her eyes to watch it, suddenly the woman sat up and smiled at her! Then she knew her hour had come. There was no escape! John was far out of hearing, and flight was impossible.

For an instant the thought of what was before her turned her almost faint, and she sank down on a log to gather up her scattered courage.

Presently she heard footsteps rustling through the withered leaves of the oak wood, and looking up there it was, standing on the edge of the wood. But now she was more than ready. Springing to her feet she advanced warily to meet it, and, when they were near enough, each sprang at the throat of the other.

Once more she felt those slender, cool, smooth fingers with their loathsome suggestion of uncanny sliminess, but this time they were clutching her throat, not merely fumbling at it; and, as her fingers sank into the throat of the Cube, the flesh, firm as it was, made her think of sinister depths of treacherous fresh water.

Then began a terrible battle. The two clung together, swaying with the fierceness of their struggles to choke each other, and the fingers of the Cube sank deeper and deeper into Daphne's flesh, while its eyes strove to force her eyes down before them with a fearful determined power, all the more ghastly because they were the very eyes she saw in her own face, whenever she looked in the glass.

And so they fought on, until at last Daphne's lids began to sink. They fell. She lost sight of her enemy, and felt it was all over, as the clutch on her throat tightened shutting off her breath. But just on the verge of the end the thought that this loathsome Thing was casting her down to annihilation stung her to one last supreme effort. Fiercely she labored to raise her heavy lids, weighed down by the gaze of the Cube. She fought with her whole heart, her whole strength. At first in vain, but at last, although with many pauses and sinkings-back, she slowly and painfully forced them up, and again met the intense purposeful glare of the Cube. Could she hold out against it, and be able to stand for another second that choking grip upon her throat?

It seemed hours that by mere force of will she held her eyelids up, and bent the whole energy of her being to forcing down those fearful eyes; but at last she saw a faint hint of doubt, almost of fear steal into them. Desperately she hung on, until there came a faint quiver of its eyelids. Were they falling? Yes! Slowly, as if weighed down by an irresistible power, they sank over its eyes, and, although at once they flew up again, this was enough. Wonderfully heartened she threw into her gaze reserves of power undreamed of before, and once more its eyelids fell; and down she held them in spite of its desperate struggles to lift them again.

Then—then at last she felt the clutch on her throat relaxing, and, as her strength returned, threw it all into the grip of her fingers, which each instant sank deeper into the flesh of the accursed Thing, while its grasp slackened, until its fingers dropped away from her throat.

Its face turned black. Its tongue protruded; and, when at length the death-rattle sounded in its throat, it was hanging a limp flaccid mass from her hands.

Then she fainted.

When John, hurrying up the hill, found her lying there he did all he could think of to bring her to herself, and succeeded at last with the help of some snow, that he found in the woods.

As she first opened her eyes, she cried out:

"Where is it?" looked around fearfully, and even tried to struggle to her feet, but when she caught sight of John she sank back with a sigh of relief, and her eyes closed once more.

In a few minutes she was able to sit up, and, as she was very thirsty, John ran down to the creek for some water, after she made him promise not to go out of sight. Then she noticed that her right hand was tightly clenched, and opening it found there a little dry shrivelled piece of flesh, and in this read a sure proof of her victory. She buried it under the dead leaves, and after she had stamped it well into the soft earth, the relief was so great that soon she felt well enough to start for home.

It was a long, hard walk for her, however, and she could barely drag herself along even with frequent rests and John's tender care and help; so he did not dare to tell her that the cake of ice was empty, when at last, it drifted out of the gorge, as he naturally supposed anxiety for the poor woman had caused Daphne's fainting-fit.

When at last they reached home, she was so exhausted that her mother put her to bed at once; but the long night's sleep brought a wonderful change in her; and a day of rest with, still more, the hope that her troubles were over made her so well that by evening she ventured on the experiment of being alone for a minute; and as this brought no sign of the double, the next day she passed a whole hour alone without being molested, and now that she was certain the Cube was gone, her health and spirits came back with a rush, and were even more buoyant and overflowing than ever before.

After Easter, when there was another party, she was eager to go, before her mother had even thought of urging it. As, early in the evening she was standing with a group of girls, she found herself shuddering violently, and felt there was something uncanny and sinister behind her. On turning she saw Eben Trissell coming toward her, and an unerring instinct told her he was a Cube. Then it flashed through her mind that three years ago Eben had suffered from a mysterious illness, which now she realized with horror was the attack of a cube, and in the struggle the true Eben must have succumbed, leaving the Cube in his place. As she shrank from the transformed Cube with loathing, his eyes grew full of terror, and he seemed to shrink together.

"You know me," he whispered. "I must go! I must go! For no Cube will ever dare to cross your path again."

He hurried from the room; and she heard later that the next day he had gone to Texas, and she never laid eyes on him again.

When she came to think over the Eben Trissell affair, the most surprising part of it was that the Cube did not differ from the original Eben Trissell in any respect, but during all those three years was the same excellent and desirable member of society, so that his real nature was revealed to her enlightened eyes alone.

It was not more than two months after this that Daphne and John were—. But this has nothing to do with the story.

Sister Hannah

I passed the year after my graduation from College in the Law School, although I had no intention of practising law or, for that matter, any other profession. The truth was I had a wild notion that some little knowledge of the law might help me in the management of my property; but long before the end of the year I got that bee out of my bonnet, and also found without the slightest question that the law was not for me, or I was not for the law.

Even in the early spring I began to talk of the coming vacation as my last, "because I must take up the serious business of life in the autumn," or at any rate come to a decision whether I should take up any business at all, or knock about the world for a year or two. On the whole I inclined to the idea of plunging into work, as I found this added a decided zest to my plans for this "last" vacation. So I put a great deal of time and thought into trying to find the most attractive way of spending it, and in the end decided to take a journey on horseback through northern New England.

Rather to my surprise there was no hitch in my plans; and the journey began quite as pleasantly as I had hoped, except for the country inns. How I did suffer from them! At that time they had reached their very lowest ebb and were marvels of shabbiness and discomfort, because the stagecoaches had vanished long ago, and motor cars were not heard of till many a year afterward.

By far the worst I came across was in an unfrequented part of New Hampshire far from any railroad. That morning, in spite of a

black and threatening sky, I had left quarters with nothing to rec-
ommend them, and pushed on, paying no attention to little spurts
of rain, until about noon the scattered showers changed into a soak-
ing downpour, and drove me to take refuge in the public house of
a little village. The stale rancid smell which met me in the doorway, would have driven me out again, if the rain pelting on my
hack had not convinced me that in such a storm it was better to
make even a port like this.

What a hole it was! I shudder even now when I think of those
meals— Well! the less said about them the better! And then that
long dreary afternoon in the close fetid bar! Time after time I decided I must get out of it, only to glance at the streaming windows,
and realize a start might land me in nearly as bad quarters (there
could not be worse) with the added misery of a thorough ducking.
As to the bed—one look at it was enough, and I passed the whole of
that wretched endless night perched on a hard, uncompromising
wooden chair. How I longed for the sunrise! And, when at last it
came, what a relief it was to look out on a bright morning washed
clean by last night's rain. I had begun to doubt if anything could
ever be clean again.

I was glad enough to shake off the dust of the inn, so far as it
was possible; and, as I rode down the village street beneath its arch-
ing elms, I breathed in great draughts of the clear clean air to try
and drive the fustiness out of my lungs. My horse had evidently
fared much better than I, and after such light work the day before
was in uproarious spirits, so, when a boy with a drum came out of
one of the last houses in the village, he laid back his ears, arched
his back, and broke into a spanking gallop. I, too, was quite ready
for a scamper, so I gave him his head, and we must have run nearly
a quarter of a mile before he shied at nothing, so far as I could see,
and getting into a mud puddle slipped, and fell, throwing me
against a stone wall with such force that I was completely stunned.

When I came to myself, I was dimly conscious of some one
bending over me, and faintly heard a woman's voice, as if at a great
distance, saying:

"We ought to carry him into the house."

And the muffled answer:

"No! Elizabeth. No! We can't do that."

"But Mehitable," said the first voice, "it seems as if he were kinder sent to us by Providence. We must take him in. We cannot let him lie here."

The other sighed deeply.

"Well! If you say so, I suppose we must, so call Ann and—"

Here I dropped off again and must have been unconscious a long time, as, when at last I came to my senses, I found I had been put to bed. As I opened my eyes, a most attractive old lady got up from a rocking-chair nearby, and told me that I must not try to talk, as I had had a serious accident, but I was in good hands, and would be well taken care of.

There was no doubt about the accident. My left arm had been broken, and an injury to my head was, I believe, even worse, although I was never entirely clear as to its nature, but suspect I understood it quite as well as the village doctor. If, however, the doctor left much to be desired, I was most fortunate in my kind hostesses, the Misses Hastings, for I could not have fallen upon more devoted care, or more comfortable quarters.

Their father, as I heard later, had been the beloved physician of this whole region, and after his death, now almost twenty years ago, his daughters had come to this retired house about a quarter of a mile from the village, and had lived here ever since. In the long hours I passed in bed I often speculated on the reason for this. It certainly was very inconvenient in many ways, especially as the two dear old ladies were the great people of the place. They visited the poor and the sick, presided at choir practice, managed the church sewing society, and in all other ways were the undisputed leaders of the village activities. Why then should they prefer to carry on all this business at arm's length, instead of living in the village itself?

The part of Lady Bountiful suited them to perfection; and, when they spoke of "the villagers" in a tone, which implied "the tenantry," if I felt inclined to smile, it was a kindly smile, as this innocent pride added a last quaint touch to their gracious and charming personalities. I, at least, had reason to be grateful to it, for, when I had offered to relieve them of the burden of my presence, as soon as I could be moved, Miss Elizabeth had said:

"No! The villagers are very good people, and would do their best for you, but none of them know how to take care of a gentleman. You will stay here."

I was only too glad to do so, as it was not at all likely that I should be so comfortable with one of "the villagers," even at the very best, and, when I thought of that perfectly impossible tavern, I shuddered to think what the worst might be.

Later, however, when I thought I was well enough to travel as far as the nearest town, where decent quarters might be found, I offered once more to go away, rather, I confess, as a matter of form than with any idea that my offer would be accepted, So imagine my disappointment, when Miss Mehitable thanked me, and said she thought I had better go! This was a cruel blow, but it brought its own remedy in the shape of a relapse, which sent me back to bed for nearly a week; and after that they would not hear of my leaving them, until I was entirely well.

Getting well was far from unpleasant. While I was confined to the house, I could enjoy the beautiful views from the windows, and the thought of the delightful walks in the woods they promised later, while before I grew strong enough, there would be long lazy days in the garden at the back of the house. This had a tantalizing air of mystery, since it was cut off from the outside world by a solid fence nearly fifteen feet high. What could be the need of such a fence? Once, when I asked Miss Elizabeth about it, she seemed much more embarrassed than the occasion called for, and after a great deal of hesitation at last could find nothing better to say than "We are fond of our privacy."

When I was well enough to go into the garden it appeared its only door opened from the house, and was locked; and, the key could not be found for half an hour, and then only after a decided flurry in the household. The garden itself, after I succeeded in getting through its defenses, was very pleasant—full of clove-pinks, sweet Williams, larkspurs, southern wood, and such old-fashioned plants arranged with a delicate grace and even a sportive fancy most unlike the primness, I should have expected from the Misses Hastings, but I could not see why either these flowers, charming as they were, or the fruit, of which there was but little, should need such exaggerated protection, for, even if they had been much better worth stealing, there were no thieves in this idyllic region.

The next time I asked to go into the garden, the key was not to be found; and, as I saw that for some unexplained reason my visits to it were unwelcome to my kind hostesses, I did not try again; and afterwards when I was able to take longer walks, I ceased to regret the fenced-in garden.

At about this time I made the acquaintance of "the villagers," and became a lion for the first and last time in my life. The coming of a stranger was more than an event, it was an adventure in their quiet secluded lives, and they made such good use of it that I was nearly swamped with invitations.

Among the first of these was one from Miss Sims, the village mantua-maker. To my great delight there were many of these quaint old-fashioned words common in our village. She received me in great state, wearing her black mitts until we sat down to tea; and after I had done what justice I could to her eight sorts of cake and other delicacies, and we had nearly finished, she suddenly fired the question at me:

"What do you think of the Misses Hastings' sister Hannah?"

"Their sister Hannah!" said I. "What do you mean? Have they got a sister?"

"Yes they hey," said she. "Hain't you seen her yet?"

"Seen her? You don't mean to say she is at home. But that is too absurd! There is not a soul in the house, but Miss Mehitable, Miss Elizabeth, and Ann."

"Do tell!" said she. "Well! I did hear as Hannah was kep' powerful close, but I had no idee it was so close, as all that comes to."

Here I realized that, supposing the Misses Hastings had a secret, it was not for me to pry into it; and I tried to turn the conversation, but it was no use until Miss Sims had told me everything she knew. This was little enough, and stripped of guesses and exaggerations came to this: The suppositious Miss Hastings, about twenty years old, was a half-sister of my two friends, and had always lived in the greatest seclusion, her very existence being concealed as far as possible. Miss Sims herself had never seen her, but the few who had said she was "uncommon hahnsome."

As I walked home that night I did my best not to think of this possible secret, but the more I tried the more I dwelt upon it, and I could not help remembering many things which might show that there was someone else in the house beside the two old ladies and their hard-featured Yankee servant Ann. For instance, more than once I had heard someone walking about in the upper story when I was sure that all the acknowledged members of the family were downstairs. Then, too, every evening after dark one of the three women took a long walk; and, when I had offered my escort to one of the ladies, it had been refused with great embarrassment. Further—and this was the most striking thing I had noticed—one day I found on the sitting-room table a strange work box, very different from the prim business-like box of either of the ladies, or the capacious ark with which Ann did the family mending. This was dainty, almost coquettish, and I felt sure must belong to a charming young girl. While I was looking at it, Miss Elizabeth came in, and after a second or two of half-frightened hesitation succeeded in finding an obviously transparent pretext for calling my attention away from the box, hid it behind her back, and then scuttled out of the room entirely forgetting her usual quiet primness.

I spent most of that night and the next day in thinking of the possible Sister Hannah, and all the time my conscience kept insisting that I ought to go away, before I intruded further; but it was so hard to leave the dear old ladies and such pleasant quarters, that I was still trying to find an excuse for avoiding this unpleasant duty, when a decision was forced on me.

The next afternoon I started on one of the long walks, now my principal amusement, but, as the day was close and sultry, and my arm unusually painful, after walking a few minutes I gave it up and went home again. The sitting room looked so cool and inviting

that I turned into it, and had reached the middle of the room, before I realized I was not alone. Seated in a rocking chair by the
shaded window was a young girl, and, although I saw only her back,
her graceful slender figure in its well-fitting blue dress, and her
thick coil of yellow hair made a most attractive picture. On the
window-sill at her elbow stood the work-box. This then was the
mysterious Sister Hannah; but, as I realized this, I saw also that if
possible, I ought to escape before she found out I was there, and
in trying to do this I must have made noise enough to attract her
attention, for she sprang from her chair, turned toward me—and
vanished!

I could not believe my eyes! She was gone, absolutely gone!

I ran to the window—no one!

As I stood gazing at the empty chair in blank astonishment, I
heard a stifled little laugh from the other side of the room, and the
door was shut gently.

What did it mean?

Could I possibly have imagined the whole thing? But no! It was
too vivid and detailed for that, and, besides, there by the window
still lay the telltale work-box.

What did it mean?

This question I asked myself over and over again all the afternoon, and was as far from an answer as ever, when I went down to
tea. There the sight of Miss Mehitable and Miss Elizabeth reminded
me of my obligations to them, and I was thoroughly ashamed that
I could have forgotten them even for a minute. My only excuse was
that the strangeness of my experience had driven everything else
out of my head.

They seemed to be quite aware I had something to tell them;
but I was kept silent by the fear that I might hurt their feelings, if
I spoke without the most careful preparation, and, therefore, as
soon as tea was over I bade them good night without a word about
the encounter of the afternoon, to their very evident disappointment. I vowed to myself, however, they should have an explanation the first thing in the morning, and was only sorry that they
would have to wait till then.

That night after I had carefully planned what I meant to say to the two old ladies, I lay awake a long time thinking disconsolately that this explanation would undoubtedly drive me away from these friends, who had become so dear to me, and a good deal to my surprise I found my, thoughts were also dwelling continually on that graceful little figure and mass of yellow hair, and that I could not bear the thought of going away without seeing them again.

Next morning at breakfast, when I said I had something important to tell them, they showed no surprise, and after the meal— I, at least, had little appetite for it—they ushered me into the awful, but somewhat musty stateliness of the parlor, and there, after we were seated, I said:

"By accident I seem to have come upon a secret of yours and have decided the only thing for me to do is to go away at once. I mean to start today for the nearest town, and I am now well enough to reach it without danger to my health."

"Thank you!" said Miss Mehitable. "Elizabeth and I knew you would act in the kindest and most considerate way. I cannot tell you how sorry we are to have you go, but really, we can find nothing else to do."

So, after telling them how I hated to say goodbye, I went upstairs to pack.

Packing with a broken arm is slow work at best, but it becomes slower than slow, when after putting each of your belongings into the valise you sit for half an hour brooding over the bad luck, which obliges you to go away, so it was within half an hour of the noon dinner time when at last I got it done, and came downstairs. The door of the parlor was open, and there sat the Misses Hastings with an air of flurried importance. They called to me to come in, and Miss Mehitable, now and then catching her breath a little as she spoke, told me:

"Elizabeth and I have been talking it over, and she says it seems as if Providence had kinder sent you to us, so (I hope it is wise) we have decided to tell you about our dear Sister Hannah."

Here is the story and I wish I could give it in her words: Their father, when he was already an old man, married as his second wife a girl several years younger than his daughters; and then after a few months of happiness their misfortunes began. A paralytic stroke changed Dr. Hastings from a hale old man into a feeble invalid; and, when they were beginning to get over this blow, and the birth of a child should have brought back happiness to them, it turned out instead an even greater misfortune, for, when Miss Mehitable laid the baby in the cradle, it vanished completely. While they were staring at the empty cradle in blank amazement, the shrieks of the young mother called them to her side. The shock had been too much for her, and she fell into convulsions, which ended in her death less than half an hour later. This double loss prostrated Dr. Hastings with a second attack so alarming that his daughters had no time or thought for anything else.

About three hours later, while they were still working over him, they were startled by hearing a child cry. Miss Mehitable followed the sound, and it led her to the chamber where the body of the young mother lay. As the noise came from the cradle she, put her hands into it, when she felt the child, although she could not see the slightest sign of it. To hush the pitiful crying she picked up the invisible baby, laid it across her knee, and then saw it, for, while its back was like that of any other child it was entirely invisible when looked at from in front.

The girl had never lost this strange peculiarity; and, as they had no wish to expose her to the talk of the villagers, after the death of their father, who followed his wife in less than a week, they built this house farther from prying eyes than their old home in the village street, and had brought her up here in absolute secrecy, themselves attending to her education to the best of their ability, as Miss Mehitable said bridling a little. This, I was sure, had left nothing to be desired, as the two ladies were perfect examples of the cultivated New England gentlewoman.

Miss Hannah was now eighteen, and of late they had begun to doubt, whether such a lonely existence was good for her, and to wish that she might have some companions more suited to her age than three old women.

Then my accident had thrown me into the family, but, even in the face of what seemed a direct interposition of Providence, they could not make up their minds to tell the secret, which they had guarded so jealously through all these years. In fact, after I had seen her, it took a great deal of discussion and much hesitation, before they could decide to introduce me to their sister, and ask me to stay, as long as I wished, so that she might have some youthful companionship.

After I had accepted this invitation with perhaps too much eagerness, Miss Elizabeth left the room and, coming back presently said:

"Let me introduce you to my sister, Hannah."

I bowed, although I could see no one, and a low sweet voice said:

"I suppose I must turn around, if you are to see me."

And at once that well-remembered, graceful back came into sight from the empty air before me. We sat down, and after the first natural stiffness had worn off, the time before dinner passed in pleasant talk.

There was something very touching in her voice. It was quiet and sweet, with even a little humorous appreciation of the oddity of the situation, but penetrating and coloring it all was a strong tinge of pathos showing that the strange fate, which cut her off from her kind, was always present in her thoughts. She was cheerful, often even merry, but this was all thrown into relief, like sunlight striking across clouds, by that background of pathetic isolation.

After this the time went only too quickly. The long days in the fenced-in garden were most delightful in the warm summer weather. We talked for hours in the old-fashioned arbor, for it was impossible to satisfy her eager curiosity about the great world she had never seen; or, when, tired of sitting still, we set to work on the flowers, I became the learner and caught from her that love of gardening, which has been one of the greatest pleasures of my life; or again, if our spirits boiled over, we chased one another round the flower beds, like a couple of children.

In the walks after dark I now acted as her escort; in fact, there was hardly an hour from morning till night when we were not together, so it was not surprising that after a week of this delightful life I found I was deeply in love with Hannah. What though I had never seen her? Do you have to see a bobolink to love it?

As soon as I realized my feelings, I spoke to her sisters. At first surprise overwhelmed all other feelings.

"What! That child!"

But this at once gave place to delight at my news; and so I entered upon the great happiness of my life.

There was nothing to prevent me from settling down in the farmhouse after our marriage, but it was necessary to arrange my affairs in Boston, before I cut loose from it forever, so after a fortnight of paradise I reluctantly said good-bye to Hannah, and travelled to Boston—a really terrible journey.

Beside making my arrangements there I went to Cambridge to call on my best friend, Professor Tane, who early in my college course had rescued me from a serious trouble with the dean; and, what was more to me, had succeeded in getting me out of a rather bad set, in which I had become entangled.

As I had no secrets from him, I told him the great news, and gave him an invitation from the Misses Hastings to come back with me for a visit. He was very glad to accept it, as his plans for the summer having miscarried, it had looked as if he would be obliged to pass the whole vacation in Cambridge.

When he was introduced to Hannah, he bowed to entirely the wrong part of the room to our great amusement, Hannah's merry laugh bubbling out with the rest. This broke the ice completely, and the evening passed most pleasantly.

After tea I gave Hannah several pieces of jewelry that had belonged to my mother. Among them there was one in particular—a necklace of spar beads—which would suit her to perfection, if she looked as my imagination pictured her. How I wished I could see if it really was as becoming, as I thought! She liked it as much as I did, and was so delighted with it, for she had a young girl's fondness for jewels, that she put it on and wore it the whole of the evening.

After the ladies had gone to bed, we went out on the porch for a smoke, and Professor Tane congratulated me most heartily.

"You are a very lucky fellow!" said he. "Miss Hastings is perfectly charming; but what an astonishing thing this partial invisibility is! It seems incredible. In fact, before I saw her, I thought you were trying to play off some huge practical joke on me, although it seemed hard to reconcile it with your state of mushy happiness; and even when I have seen her, or rather have not seen her, I find it hard to believe my senses. It is certainly most interesting, and"— after a pause— "I wonder if I may have found the explanation for it."

At this I was all attention.

"Did you notice," he went on, "that when she wore those spar beads you could see them?"

"Why!" said I, "why yes! I believe I did see them in an indistinct sort of way."

"I saw them plainly," said he.

And then he launched out into a long explanation, which at the time I thought I understood perfectly, but now that I try to repeat it, I find much of it is very misty. It seems that this spar (I think he called it fluor-spar) has the power of changing the color of the light, which falls upon it. For instance, it turns white light to purple, and this makes pieces that are really white look purple. Now, as we could see the beads when Hannah was wearing them, Professor Tane thought that she might give off from in front only invisible light, which in passing through the beads was turned into visible light.

Invisible light was a strange idea to me. It seemed like a contradiction in terms, but Professor Tane told me that sunlight contains a good many more of these invisible, ultraviolet rays, than of the visible ones. (That word ultraviolet has stuck in my memory anyway!) When I asked how they knew there was such a thing as invisible light, he said one way was by letting it fall on this spar, which made it into visible light, and another was by photographing it.

"So," said he, "if Miss Hannah does give off ultraviolet rays,"—

"We can photograph her!" shouted I.

"Oh! You have taken in that idea, have you?" said he "Of course we can, that is, if my explanation is the right one, but there are so many weak spots in it that I would not crow till we see if it works."

Fortunately it was easy to test it, as he had brought his photographic kit with him, and we agreed the experiment should be tried the first thing in the morning.

I got the Professor out of bed at a perfectly unearthly hour, and sent the exciting news to the ladies by Ann, whose work always began at daybreak. They soon joined us, and we waited with the utmost impatience, till the light became strong enough. Hannah was as eager as any of us, for she, poor girl, felt an intense curiosity to know what she looked like.

When at last the moment arrived, there arose the difficulty of focusing the camera upon her, but the Professor was equal to the occasion. He made a pile of books on a table beside her, focused the machine on that, and then swung it around, until it covered the chair, on which she was sitting.

I shall never forget our excitement, as we crowded round the Professor in the closet we had converted into a dark room, anxiously craning our necks to get a glimpse of the plate, nor how simply interminable the development of that plate seemed, although it could not have taken more than a few minutes. At last the image appeared, but what a disappointment! There was an excellent picture of the chair, but not the least sign of Hannah.

This blow, which destroyed his theory, seemed to crush Professor Tane. He stared at the plate in a dazed sort of way a minute or so, and then struck himself a tremendous blow on the forehead.

"I ought to resign my professorship," said he. "I am not fit to teach chemistry in a primary school."

"Why! What is the matter?"

"Matter enough! Glass absorbs the ultraviolet rays, so none of them could get through the lens."

"Then we must give it up?"

"O no! Not at all! They pass easily through quartz, and luckily I happen to have a very good quartz lens."

"Oh! Let us try it at once!" we all cried, but he answered sadly:

"It is in Cambridge."

However, he was certainly most obliging, for after only one day of rest he took that terrible journey again; and came back as soon as he could have the quartz lens fitted to his camera, so that our suspense lasted only a few days.

Then came the sitting as before, and the endless waiting, while he developed the plate, but even that was done at last, and for the first time we all saw Hannah. There she sat, or rather half of her, for the Professor had turned the camera a little too far, but that was no matter, as here was the proof that we could photograph her, and before night we had a great many good pictures, and knew how she looked almost as well as if we could see her in the ordinary way.

How can I describe her demure, pathetic charm, lighted by a gleam of fun playing in her eyes? But why should I try? No words could make you see her, or bring before you her fresh sweet New England beauty.

That evening, as we were smoking on the porch, I congratulated Professor Tane on the confirmation of his theory, and he certainly did seem pretty well pleased with himself.

He then told me that we could come even nearer to making Hannah visible, as there were several other things, which like the spar change invisible into visible light, and, as some of them are taken up by water, if we bathed her face and dress in them, we ought to be able to see her actually.

I was so delighted at this that I jumped up, and shook his hand vigorously, but I suppose my raptures must have been too much for him, as he at once spoilt my pleasure by telling me that the best we could do would be to make her bright sky blue, or vivid parrot green.

In spite of this, however, I decided that we ought to try the experiment, because the little knowledge of law I had picked up in the Law School was proving, if not a dangerous, at least an uncomfortable thing. I learned then that a marriage to be legal must take place in the presence of witnesses, but would this be the case when the witnesses could see only part of Hannah?

This doubt was absurd, I imagine, but, as we could not be too careful, we made up our minds after some discussion to try to make Hannah visible on the wedding day. Good-natured Professor Tane offered to go to Boston again to get the things that we needed, but we were not inhuman enough to ask him to start at once, so he passed a pleasant week at the farmhouse, and then ventured once more on that most repulsive journey.

Before he started for Cambridge, he said to me:

"You will not want to have the villagers chattering about your bride, as they certainly will, if you have the village minister, so why wouldn't it be a good plan to get my classmate, Forrest, to marry you? He has a parish in Nashua, and, as he is unmarried, there will be no danger that the secret will leak out through him."

I was amused that he should have learned already to speak of the villagers as we do, but I must say, too, that I thought he need not be jeering at women all the time, even if he is such a confirmed old bachelor.

Two days before the wedding, when Professor Tane came back with his pleasant friend, Mr. Forrest, he was in high feather, for he told us a new chemical—Magdala red—had been discovered, which would make a very good flesh color, and he had been lucky enough to get some of it for Hannah's face and hands. So all the next morning he was very busy making this wash for Hannah, and two others, in which Ann was to soak the wedding dress and veil.

Of course, I was not allowed to see her until the ceremony, but, when she came into the parlor my fears of legal difficulties vanished completely, for you could see her, I must confess a little vaguely and indistinctly, but she was visible without the slightest question. I cannot say much for the flesh color of which Professor Tane was so proud. I should call it a pale brick red, but then it looked much better for her face and hands than the sky blue of the dress, or the bright yellowish green of the veil.

It was a great pleasure really to see her, but I have never repeated the experiment, although Professor Tane was kind enough to give me a good supply of each of the washes. To tell the truth the effect was a trifle ghastly, and beside I do not want to run any risk of hurting my wife's complexion.

These proofs of Professor Tane's theory were enough for me, but evidently they did not satisfy him, for some years later, when the Roentgen rays were discovered, he came to me with a new one, which, he said, explained some facts in Hannah's case that were not in harmony with his first theory. I took little interest in it, however, for even if I could have understood it, I feel that Hannah is far too sacred to be made an object of study.

Since our marriage my life has run on quietly, but most happily in the farmhouse. I have devoted myself to photography, and have probably the finest quartz lenses in the world, so that now my collection of over three thousand photographs of Hannah makes me nearly as familiar with her, as if I could see her always.

None of our children, I am happy to say, take after their mother, but I noticed that, when the older children asked "Where is Mamma?" our second girl, Lizzie, could always point her out. This led me to ask Professor Tane to examine her eyes, and he found that she could see the ultraviolet rays, which was a most fortunate discovery for her, as she had always been nearly blinded by the sunlight, and no wonder, poor child, since for her it was more than twice as bright as for the eyes of us common people. The trouble was remedied by spectacles made of window glass, which cut off the ultraviolet rays, and with these she can bear the sun as well as any one.

So my life glides away. People may wonder how I can bear to be so entirely cut off from all the rest of the world, but I do not miss it, for Hannah is all the world to me.

Linden

It began when Stendal had his hair cut. Mine needed it much more, but he found the barber's shop so revolting that I decided to wait till next time, and then there was not any next time, for after this our work led us through villages, or small towns, where, if they had a barber's shop, one glance at it drove me across the street to get as far from it as I could. Filthy holes!

After nearly a month of this sort of thing I grew most outrageously frowsy. Stendal told me I looked like a Welsh bard, or a druid, but I knew better. I was frowsy. And at last I told him we must go to some city, where I could have my hair cut decently. When he had agreed grudgingly enough, we crossed into Switzerland, as the nearest large city was there, and soon after we had passed the frontier, stopped at a junction, where we had to change cars.

Here a polite man offered to show us our train. He was not in uniform, so at first I thought he could not be an official, but when I saw one of his fingers was bandaged, I had my doubts, because I had grown to think this almost as much the badge of a railroad man as the regulation cap.

He led us over platform after platform, until at last I began to wonder, if he were taking us to the right train, and asked Stendal what he thought, but to my surprise got no answer, and looking at him, saw that he seemed to be in a sort of trance walking with his eyes riveted on our guide with a queer unseeing, faraway expression. When I started to speak again a strange quiescence stole over me, which made speaking such an intolerable effort, that I, too, walked on in silence, until presently our guide opened the door of a compartment, and pointed into it with his bandaged hand. Stendal stumbled in, I followed, and was glad enough to slump into a corner, as I was overwhelmed with sleep, and looking drowsily across at Stendal saw that he was already nodding in the opposite corner.

When I came to myself, I had no idea where I was, or how I got there; and, as I grew more wide awake, instead of solving this puzzle, I only grew more muddled. I had gone to sleep in a railway carriage. That I knew. How then could I be here undressed and in bed? Stendal, who was just waking up in a bed on the other side of the room, knew where we were no more than I; and the time, since we left the junction was a complete blank to both of us, although our watches, which were under our pillows, told us it was more than three hours.

The room in which we were lying seemed to be a bed-chamber in a good hotel of the second class, but how did we get there? Jumping out of bed we ran to the window in the hope of finding out where we were, but the view from it gave us no help. It looked out on a good-sized square with a large building, evidently a church, directly opposite. Its architecture was Gothic, but with strange bizarre details in its construction and ornamentation, utterly unlike anything we had ever seen before, which lent it a quaint mysterious charm. The same attractive outlandishness appeared in the houses on the square, and also in the dress of the few people in sight. In this common-place age it was refreshing to find costumes universal and picturesque.

With our curiosity only whetted, we turned back into the room, and then noticed for the first time that our clothes had been neatly folded, and piled on two chairs, and our valises were standing open, after our night shirts had been taken out of them, but a careful search showed that nothing was missing. What could it mean?

We began to dress quickly to find someone who could clear up this astonishing puzzle, but before we had finished, a loud noise as of many people shouting in unison drew us again to the window, where we saw gathered before the doors of the church, a large crowd, which, as we reached the window again poured forth, this chant or measured shouting, and, as they repeated it a third time, the doors flew open, and a few of them entered the church, followed in a minute by the rest.

The language of the chant was a German patois so strange and uncouth that we could not have understood it, if we had not been so familiar with German, and, as it was, we had our doubts, for when we turned back to our dressing, Stendal asked:

"Does not 'Zehen' mean toes?"

"It certainly does," said I. "But what did they mean by, 'Give us the toes! Give us the toes!'"

We could make nothing of it.

When at last we went downstairs, we found we were in a fair hotel of the second class, better on the whole than those we had encountered in the latter part of our journey. The landlord, a large, rather genial man, told us that the town was called Linden, and had been founded by a religious reformer of that name for his disciples, who had lived here for many centuries, almost completely shut off from the rest of the world.

Stendal then asked:

"What did the people mean by shouting, 'Give us the toes?'"

At once our host's mouth shut like a clam, and he glowered at us full of doubt and suspicion. Not another word could we get out of him, and this was unlucky, as we had not yet found how we came to Linden. He left us almost at once, and sent in his son, a handsome boy of fifteen or sixteen, to bring us our supper; but we made nothing out of him, as he knew only waiter's German, and questions not connected with the table were answered by floods of the Linden patois—unintelligible in such torrents as so much Choctaw. After going to our room we discussed the mystery the whole evening, but were as far from an explanation as ever, when we went to bed.

The next morning we explored the town, and were delighted with it. As it lay in the midst of a cup-shaped valley, the view down each street was closed by snow-capped mountains, bizarre and picturesque

details, like those in the church, were frequent enough in the common houses to keep our interest on the stretch, and the costumes
and manners of the people were as strange and interesting, as was
to be expected from the isolation in which they lived.

Early in our walk we noticed a large number of men with bandaged hands, and, at first, supposed they were caused by some
dangerous trade peculiar to the town, but after we had counted
twenty-two in half an hour, it seemed they could hardly be acci-
dental, and we grew certain they were not, when we found that
only the little finger of the left hand was bandaged, except in two
cases where the ring finger also was bound up. Beside this instead
of being made of common white cloth, the bandages had a distinct
greenish color. On this I turned to Stendal, and saw by his startled
look that the same thought had struck both of us.

The man at the junction!

"His bandage was greenish white," said I.

"And on the little finger of his left hand," added Stendal.

What did it mean?

That morning we found nothing more, except that these bandaged men evidently belonged to an upper class, as all the others
bowed to them with profound respect, many even standing uncovered until they had passed.

At the mid-day dinner we asked the landlord about the bandaged finger.

"It is," said he, "the badge of an ecclesiastical aristocracy
founded by Linden."

"A queer badge!" said I. "And it must be very inconvenient. Why
should they bind up a perfectly sound finger?"

But at this his suspicions shut his mouth just as on the day
before, and we were thrown back on what we could find out by
ourselves to clear up the mystery.

In the afternoon we were fortunate enough to see two incidents,
which showed that these bandaged aristocrats were possessed of
some unusual power or powers. Two carts had met in a narrow
street, where there was no room to pass, and each driver, refusing

to back his horse, a quarrel started which threatened to grow into something like a small riot, as the bystanders joined one or the other party. At this moment one of the bandaged men came down the street, and when he saw the trouble, raised his left hand. The effect was almost magical. The angry tumult stopped short. Each carter began backing out of the deadlock, and as the crowd dispersed, we heard them saying:

"Oh, the good mutilate! The excellent man!"

Later, as the dusk was closing in, we were following a mutilate through a shabby lane, bordered on one side by back yards, when from one of them a savage dog sprang at him, but he raised his bandaged hand, and, if we could believe our eyes, the dog stopped short in the midst of its spring, cowered for an instant at his feet, and then slunk off with its tail between its legs.

Two or three days passed quietly after this without throwing any more light on the mystery; and yet we lingered in the town, although we had exhausted its sights completely; but a peaceful laziness bound us to the out-of-the-world little place so firmly that leaving it called for an effort beyond our powers.

During this time, however, we did find out, why Linden had such a good hotel, although it had little or no intercourse with the outer world. It was, we learned, kept up for the benefit of the commercial travellers, who supplied the town with the many necessities, which the people could not produce for themselves. One of these men arrived a day or two later, and the following morning when we started for our walk, exclaimed:

"But that is absolutely forbidden!" and could not get over his astonishment, when he found that we were allowed to walk freely in the town, as he and his like were strictly confined to the hotel.

As time went on, we began to wonder at the sensation we caused. Where strangers were such rarities, they would of course be stared at, but hardly run after and thronged upon, as we were; and curiously enough as the people grew more familiar with us, this sensation instead of wearing off, as would have been expected, became even more marked. Luckily their feeling toward us was not

hostile, on the contrary it was distinctly friendly, even respectful,
many of them standing uncovered while we passed, as if we had
been mutilates.

One day, when we were talking this over in our room, Stendal said:

"I suppose you realize it is your *beaux yeux* which bring us all
this admiration."

At first I supposed he was only jeering at my frowsy appearance, but he insisted seriously that I was the object of interest,
and to prove it told me to stand at the window, while he walked
across the square alone; and when he came back I was obliged to
confess that he had been stared at even less than I should have
expected. Then he added:

"Have you noticed that the landlord will answer all your questions, but has not a word for mine?"

This also I doubted, but we tried the experiment at dinner, and
found that while a question asked by Stendal was received only
with a surly glare; if I repeated it in the same words, the landlord
was ready enough to give me a full and courteous answer. I took
advantage of this to extract more information from him, and found
that we had been mistaken in supposing Linden a mere religious
reformer. Instead, his disciples believed he was a divine being—a
demigod at the least—and worshipped him with most intense devotion.

His teachings had been preserved with religious care for the
four centuries since his death. Chief among them were prophecies
of a glorious second coming, after an appointed cycle had passed,
when he would return to spread his empire over the whole earth. I
was particularly interested in finding the Messianic belief crop-
ping up in this obscure religion, as it has always been my favorite
study.

The landlord told us also that on the next day began the holy
week of the Lindenites, which was celebrated with many imposing
ceremonies; but, when I asked whether we could see them, he
looked at me strangely, and answered gruffly that he thought not;
and then his increasing doubt and suspicion struck him obstinately
dumb.

The next morning we presented ourselves at the door of the church in good time, as we were determined not to lose the services, if we could help it. At first two mutilates were inclined to bar our way, but almost immediately they thought better of it, and let us pass with marked politeness.

The inside of the church, unlike its exterior, was bare and plain. There was little or no ornament, and it was without dignity in spite of its great size. Most of the floor was loosely set with cane-bottomed chairs arranged on each side of a broad central aisle, and across the further end of this stood the only pew, which was richly and elaborately carved in strong contrast with the extreme plainness of everything else. Beyond this pew was a large open space, and against the further wall of the church something that looked like an altar, except that it was too low, and covered with black cloth. Above it hung a large picture, or rather a heavily carved frame surrounding a canvass so black with age that not a vestige of the design could be made out.

After we had waited some time, a procession appeared from a door in this further wall. First came six priests magnificently dressed, who, as they marched, held their hands crossed upon their breasts, showing bandages on the little and ring fingers of their left hands. Then followed a man well past middle age, whose gray hair only intensified the malignant power which showed in every line of his cruel face. I had never seen a personality more impressive and forbidding. His vestments were even richer than those of the attendant priests, and as his hands were also crossed upon his breast, we could see that every one of his fingers was swathed in a greenish bandage. Six priests, like the first following him, closed the procession.

As it reached the middle of the open space, and turned to face the congregation, all the people fell upon their knees, and bowed their heads with almost exaggerated devotion. Then one of the attendants advanced, and kneeling before the chief priest held up to him a large open volume, and from this living lectern he read in a loud and solemn voice, while a second attendant stood ready to turn the pages, as he could not do it for himself with his bandaged fingers. We understood little of his reading. The language was even ruder than that now spoken in Linden, and the subject matter was so unintelligibly mystical that even I could not understand it, in spite of my taste for studies of that kind. We were much relieved, therefore, when at last it came to an end.

As the two priests retired with the book, the others also withdrew, and ranged themselves against the wall, leaving the chief priest alone in the middle of the open space. A mutilate, now arising from the pew of honor, came forward and held up his bandaged finger, and the chief priest began a strange waving motion with his hands. He seemed to grasp some invisible thing out of the air, and drawing it toward him stored it up within his body, until at last he turned all his bandaged fingers upon the other's hand like a battery of guns concentrated on a single target. What happened next I should not dare to tell, if Stendal did not confirm me in every particular; but, as we gazed, a pale greenish light appeared playing between the bandaged fingers of the two men; at first hardly visible in the broad daylight, it slowly grew more intense, until we saw clearly a phosphorescent ray, or rather band of light shining between their hands. Soon the mutilate's bandage began to blacken, next it smoked, and at last burst into flame, and burnt away leaving the stump of the little finger bare. After this three priests approached, one of whom carried bandages, the second a number of small white objects on a silver platter, and the third bound one of these on the uncovered stump. The mutilate then returned to his seat, and another took his place.

This ceremony was repeated over and over again; and, striking as it was at first, we soon became thoroughly weary of it, but escape was impossible, as the whole congregation hung upon it with a hushed devotional intensity that we could not dream of disturbing.

As we saw it nine or ten times, we were able to take in even small details. We observed, for instance, that the bandaged finger was very clumsy, even club-like at first, but slender and tapering after the rebandaging; also that the burning of the bandage must have been extremely painful. During it the sweat started out on the faces of the mutilates, few of them were determined enough to repress a violent shuddering, and some, as we could see, kept themselves from screaming only by using the last particle of their self-control; but after his finger had been bound up again, each returned to his seat with a look of the most peaceful beatitude. One thing, however, baffled us. We could not make out the nature of the white objects bound on the fingers of the mutilates, even although we strained our eyes to the uttermost.

Long after our patience had been exhausted, the tedious service came to an end, and we were glad enough to join the worshippers in streaming out of the church.

At dinner our landlord told us, or I should say me, for as before he had no words for Stendal, that the ceremony was a promotion of the mutilates from the lowest to a higher class, and was called "the changing of the joints." This I got out of him with some difficulty—oddly enough, not because he was unwilling to talk, but because he seemed to think that I was already thoroughly familiar with the whole ceremony, and in the end he gave me the information, as if he felt it necessary to humor an incomprehensible whim of mine. When he spoke of changing joints and I echoed,

"The joints?"

He answered with some irritation,

"The sacred joints, of course!"

And when I asked,

"And what are the sacred joints?"

He started, as if I had struck him. Astonishment, perplexity, and doubt chased each other over his face, which settled at last into angry suspicion, and then nothing would break his dogged silence.

Fortunately he had told us before this that the next day was devoted to still more impressive ceremonies; and, as we were determined not to miss them, we were early at the church; but, early as we were, it was already crowded, and we secured seats only through the kind offices of a mutilate, who found two for us, which were near the door, but on the broad central aisle, so that we could see very well.

The procession, when at last it appeared, was led by six priests, as on the previous day, followed by a group of four others, two walking backward, two forward, and all pointing with their bandaged hands at a boy of about sixteen clothed in white and crowned with flowers, who moved in their midst, as if in a trance with a distant, unseeing look in his eyes, which seemed vaguely familiar, although I could not remember where I had seen it. Next came the chief priest; and the procession was closed as before by six inferior priests.

The ceremony began with a reading from the sacred volume, even more lengthy and tedious than that of the day before. When at last it came to an end, the boy, still apparently under the hypnotic influence of the four priests, stretched himself on the altar. The priests withdrew, and an expectant movement in the congregation told us something important was coming. The chief priest advanced to the altar, and once more, as in yesterday's ceremony, but with even more compelling gestures, seemed to drag power from the air, and store it up within his body, until, when at last he turned his bandaged fingers downward, dazzling flashes of vivid green lightning poured from them upon the boy, who after a convulsive shudder lay stiff and motionless—and I had seen a human sacrifice! As the truth forced itself upon me, I sprang up in horrified protest, but Stendal pulled me back into my chair.

"Steady, man! Steady!" whispered he. "Our lives hang on a hair! Pull yourself together, if we are to get out alive."

This was too true, but even to save our lives I could hardly choke back my horror and disgust. Fortunately, however, their hellish ceremony had so engrossed the people that my outbreak passed unnoticed.

Meanwhile, the chief priest had raised his head, and was gazing at the blackened picture above the body, while his bandaged hands moved back and forth across it in slow, impressive gestures. As the force flowed out from them, gradually an image began to peer through the slowly fading blackness, and grew more and more distinct, till a portrait appeared within the frame, vivid and fresh, as on the day when it was painted. It was the picture of a man in a coarse brown robe girded with a cord about his waist; his hand was raised in the act of blessing, and his strong face, partly covered with the rough hair and beard, glowed with a wonderful rapt inspiration. The whole man was almost overwhelming in his shaggy grandeur. As the chief priest bowed his head before it in adoration, the people fell on their knees, and a tense whisper:—

"Linden! Linden!" thrilled through the church.

The appearance of this astonishing picture had almost turned my thoughts from the dead body lying below, but they were recalled to it in a most shocking way. Four priests armed with knives knelt beside it, and began cutting off its fingers and toes.

The sacred joints!

This was too much for me, I sprang to my feet, and shouted:

"I will not stand it!"

At the sound the worshippers turned with an ominous rustle, and I realized we were lost. I braced myself for the rush, but it did not come. For a space the people hung back in awed indecision, and Stendal took advantage of it to seize my arm, and drag me from the church.

As we hurried down the steps, he hissed in my ear:

"My God! You are the living image of Linden!"

We ran across the square to escape the outraged worshippers, who we expected would be on our track like a swarm of hornets. Our only refuge was the hotel, and, although safety was hardly to be hoped for there, or anywhere, we made for it at the top of our speed, succeeded in reaching it, and, looking back fearfully, saw to our great surprise there was no pursuit whatever. Still we did not dare to draw breath, until we had gained our room, when with the door locked and barricaded, we summoned courage enough to look cautiously from the window.

Outside the empty square slept peacefully under the noon-day sun; and this quiet was not disturbed for several minutes, until, when the services were over at last, the people flowed out of the church, and scattered to their homes, as if nothing unusual had happened.

The immediate danger passed, the remembrance of what we had seen came over us with a sick horror, amounting almost to nausea; and this did not subside till late in the afternoon.

When at length we felt equal to discussing the situation, it was black enough. The absence of an immediate attack did not deceive us. We knew that we were doomed, since even without my sacrilege in the church, we had seen too much to be allowed to escape; and as we talked it over, it became only too plain that our fate had been sealed from the beginning, for the mutilate at the junction must have trepanned us into Linden to serve as victims in our turn.

Our escape so far was probably due to my strong resemblance to Linden, and it might explain, also, the absence of pursuit this morning, but, as we recalled the menacing personality of the chief priest, we were sure it would not protect us much longer, perhaps not even until nightfall, so our only hope was in flight. This, however, was no easy matter, for, though the hypnotic tie which had bound us to the place had been rudely broken by the sacrifice, there were great physical obstacles to be overcome. Our explorations of the town and its neighborhood had shown that no railroad came near it, and in an escape on foot, even if we could get out of the streets unnoticed, we must still pass through miles of farms and market-gardens swarming with laborers, and then, after we had reached the base of the mountains, find a pass, that would lead us between their inaccessible peaks.

After much talk we decided to make the attempt, desperate as it was, on the following day, when most of the Lindenites would be gathered in the church.

At supper time, although we shrank from leaving the comparative safety of our locked room with the danger of encountering hostile Lindenites, we were driven to it by the necessity of fortifying ourselves for the journey of the next day, especially as we had gone without dinner. To our great relief the landlord did not appear, and we saw no one but his son, a pleasant boy, of whom we had grown decidedly fond; but supper passed in complete silence, as we had nothing more to ask; we knew only too well what the sacred joints were, and even how the toes were changed for the fingers.

In the evening we made up two small bundles of necessaries that could be carried easily, as we had to leave our baggage behind; and went to bed early to sleep off the excitement and fatigue of the day. I do not know how Stendal succeeded, but I was so tormented by horrible dreams that the dawn came as a relief, and I got up entirely unrefreshed.

We dressed hastily, and were tying up our bundles, when a loud despairing shriek echoed through the house, We ran downstairs and in the middle of the dining-room saw our landlord's young son with horror frozen in his eyes glaring at two priests, who stood with their bandaged fingers levelled at him. As we looked the horror slowly faded, giving place to the vacant, far-away trance-like stare, which was even more appalling, as we thought of what it meant. Then walking backward the priests slowly moved from the room, and he followed, drawn to his death.

As the door closed behind them, I saw his mother crouching in a corner, her apron over her head, rocking to and fro in a convulsive agony of grief. The landlord sat at the table, his arms spread out upon it, and his face buried in them, while from time to time a great sob shook his heavy frame; and now I wasted much precious time trying to console them—in vain, for what can be said to the mother and father of a victim? Then all at once the Divine Fire blazed up within me.

"This accursed rite!" I cried. "I will stop it!"

And the Divine Fire ever blazing more fiercely swept me from the house and across the square, until, brushing aside the protests of Stendal, I reached the Church. The doors flew open before me and I strode into the aisle. I was almost too late. The victim was just stretching himself on the altar.

"Stop!" I thundered. "I forbid it!"

The whole great congregation with the snarl of a hungry tiger turned to crush the intruder, but even as crouching for the spring they glared at me, awe and wonder struck them motionless. All but the chief priest.

He, too, for a moment stood amazed, then his face wild with devilish fury rushed down the aisle, grasping huge stores of irresistible force out of the air, and hurling them against me in blinding lightnings, but borne on high by the Divine Fire, I felt them play harmlessly beneath my feet.

For a long minute we faced each other—and then I ended it.

I raised my hand, and the accursed priest fell dead at my feet.

At the same instant the portrait, bursting through the veiling blackness seemed almost to start from its frame, and the people fell grovelling on their faces screaming:

"Linden! Linden!"

Stendal tells me that in that supreme moment I blazed like a flame of fire.

* * * * *

Since then I have ruled alone in Linden with Stendal as my prime minister.

But am I really Linden?

At times the Divine Fire within me blazes fiercely enough to burn up all doubt; but between there are long periods of uncertainty, when I can justify myself only by remembering how much I have done for my people. I have abolished the accursed sacrifices; I have burnt the sacred joints, and such is my hold on my people that even the mutilates did not rebel; and I am slowly leading them to a higher and better faith; but I have never been able to have my hair cut.

The Travelling Companion

In the early part of the nineteenth century there lived in the north of England a substantial country gentleman named Thomas Bartram, who was entirely satisfied with "the station of life to which it had pleased God to call him." The care of his large estate, the business of quarter sessions, field sports, and the jovial sociability of the neighborhood kept him so pleasantly employed from morning to night that he would have been completely happy, if the low tastes and outrageous behaviour of his son James had not irritated and vexed him almost beyond endurance.

As a child he had been spoiled by a foolish and indulgent mother; and after her death he had been left in his early boyhood to the care of the servants, who knew it was not for them to cross the young squire in anything, and in too many cases taught him to share their own low pleasures. His father stormed at each new offence, but as this was all, and the boy was still left with the servants, things went from bad to worse, and the only result of his interference was to make his son dislike and fear him.

In fact, the boy would have grown up a complete Tony Lumpkin, if he had not been packed off to school, where he learned the dissipations, as well as the manners, of a gentleman without losing the taste for low pleasures he had brought with him from home.

When he went to the University, heavy debts were added to his other offences, and the letters that passed between him and his father soon became demands (rather than requests) for money on one side, and grudging supplies mixed with angry refusals on the other, so that the breach between them grew still wider.

His behaviour seemed all the blacker by contrast with that of Henry Mordaunt, a distant cousin, who some years before, when left a penniless orphan, had been taken in at the Hall by the Squire, and, as he was only two years older than James, the two boys had grown up together, until the young Squire was sent to school.

From the very first Mordaunt had made himself useful, and by the time James went to the University he had worked up to the complete management of the estate in fact, although not in name. He was well fitted for this post, as he was faithful and energetic, and had worked hard to develop his good natural ability in every way.

As he was, if anything, too exemplary and sober for his years, James Bartram could hardly have avoided hating him in any case, but, when the Squire never tired of holding him up as an example and wishing he had such a son, home became intolerable to the young man, and he began to spend his long vacations in a round of visits, which so offended his father that he ceased to take any notice of his letters for money, and there was nothing left for him but trading with the Jews on the prospects of his inheritance.

In the middle of his second year at the University he was startled by a letter from Henry Mordaunt calling him to the bedside of his father, if he wished to see him alive. At once he took horse, and travelled night and day, but his horse went lame, which, with a broken bridge, delayed him two full days upon the road, and he reached the Hall only to find that his father had died that morning.

Mordaunt seemed anxious to avoid him till after the funeral, but, when the time for reading the will drew near, sought him out, and told him with a great deal of embarrassment that, while his father in the earlier part of his sickness had spoken of him often with great affection, and counted the days before he could reach home, when two more days had passed, and still he did not come, the Squire had broken out in bitter reproaches, and insisted on dictating a new will to Mordaunt, which he signed at the very end, when he was so weak he could hardly hold the pen.

"I did my best to stop him," said Mordaunt, "but he would not listen to my protests. What would not I give to have it different!"

The Squire had entrusted the will to Sir Geoffrey Dunscombe, his oldest friend, who also was one of the witnesses. When read it appeared that James Bartram was cut off with a shilling, "because of many instances of undutiful behaviour," and the whole estate left to "my dearly beloved cousin, the staff of my old age, Henry Mordaunt."

This blow seemed to stun Bartram, who listened in dazed silence to Mordaunt's exclamation that it was an unjust will, and should be broken at once, but here Sir Geoffrey interrupted:

"Pshaw! My dear boy!" said he, "build no hopes on that! Henry, good fellow, is saying it only to raise your spirits, but at his request I examined the will with particular care, and you may take it on my word it cannot be broken. No, my boy! It cannot be broken."

"I am afraid that is only too true," sighed Mordaunt. "But, if it must stand in law, it shall not in fact. You, James, must take half of the estate."

But he answered sullenly:

"The money is yours. I will not touch a penny. I made my bed. It is right I should lie on it."

Mordaunt would not give it up so, and did his best to persuade Bartram to accept half the estate, or at worst a handsome allowance, but it was doubtful if he heard him. Certainly, he gave no sign of it; and at last called for his horse, and rode away from the Hall, and from that time nothing was ever heard of him. This was not surprising, as now that he was disinherited, the gates of a debtors' prison were yawning for him in London. It was supposed that he had taken refuge abroad, but as not the slightest trace of him could be found, Mordaunt had to enter on his inheritance without making any provision for the son of his benefactor.

In the care of his tenants, and the management of his estate, he proved an ideal country gentleman. At quarter sessions, too, his opinion carried great weight, and his duller and less educated neighbors looked up to him with admiration; but, although respected, he was not liked, as the seriousness, which had been so

marked even when he was a boy, developed in the man into a sombre moodiness. He took no part in the field sports of the country,
and shrank from society of every kind, which was perhaps as well,
since he was far from an enlivening companion.

This gloomy melancholy may have been due in part to ill health,
as he was far from well; and, as the years passed, his trouble grew
upon him, until he determined at last to make the journey to London, and consult one of the celebrated physicians there.

This great man was far from satisfied with his condition, and
prescribed a remedy just coming into vogue then, although common enough now, a tour on the continent, which he advised should
be made as far as possible on horseback.

As by this time the Napoleonic wars were so long passed that
travelling on the continent was open once more to Englishmen, he
sailed for Holland, and made his way from there to the borders of
France without any unusual incident.

On the day that he was approaching the frontier the afternoon
found him pushing on from Dinant to reach Givet, his quarters for
the night, before it grew dark, as he did not relish the prospect of
travelling by night, and especially on such a lonely road, where for
an hour he had seen no other passenger. At last far ahead he caught
sight of a traveller on horseback, and made up his mind to over-
take him, for he had been entirely alone for a week, and this had
driven him to such a pitch of desperation that he longed for any
companion, even if the barrier of language stood between them.
He did not decide on this without some misgivings, but, as he was
well mounted and armed, he had little to fear from only one man.

Accordingly, he set spurs to his horse, and, when near enough,
called to the other, but without any effect. A second call, when he
was still nearer, also brought no answer, so that he wondered if
the man were deaf; but at a third the traveller pulled up his horse,
and swung it round to face Mordaunt—a wise precaution in such
dangerous times—so that he had a good chance to study him carefully, as he rode up.

The stranger was a rotund little fellow, the lower part of whose
broad jolly face was curtained by a heavy black beard, which, however, could not destroy the impression of the genial humor shining

from the merry lines around his eyes and the eyes themselves, which were twinkling even now, as if he were chewing on some more than usually delicious joke.

He wore a horseman's cloak of heavy dark blue woolen stuff, long enough to protect him from rain, and warm enough to keep off the cold, but, as the afternoon was warm for the season, it was thrown back from his shoulders, showing a worn and frayed travelling dress, but, a little to Mordaunt's relief, no sign of a weapon. He rode a sorry nag in such bad case that Mordaunt was surprised it had been able to keep ahead of him for so long a time. Altogether, the man seemed in straitened circumstances, if not pinched by absolute want.

As Mordaunt came up with him, and tried to ask in his halting French, whether they might not join company, the stranger burst into a hearty laugh, and asked:

"And what is there wrong with English?"

Mordaunt could have fallen on his neck! After his week of desolating solitude to find not only a companion, but an Englishman. He felt as if he had found a brother!

Soon they were jogging along at a good pace toward Givet, as the other was also bound for that place. The stranger seemed to have travelled everywhere, and seen everything, and told his experiences in such an amusing and vivid way that Mordaunt felt, as if he were actually taking part in them. Then, too, he was full of droll stories, and punctuated his talk with such a hearty and contagious laugh that it made even the sombre Mordaunt relax into a smile.

He was especially familiar with that part of the country, and, as they neared Givet, recommended one of the two inns so warmly that Mordaunt suspected he might be laying a trap for him, as, in spite of all his jollity and good-fellowship, there was something about the man, which gave him a feeling of distrust. He did not know what it was, and yet he could not help thinking that it would be well to be on his guard. So he answered brusquely that he should go to the other inn.

"It is a poor hole," said his travelling companion; "but we can manage to stand it. You need not look so astonished at that 'we.'

Do you suppose, when I have the rare good fortune to meet an Englishman, and such a good listener too, I am going to let him slip through my fingers?"

And he laughed heartily at the idea. Now for the first time Mordaunt noticed something unpleasant about that laugh. It seemed to be made up of many strands, or threads, and, while almost all of them were jovial, merry, or even uproarious, there was one, that was distinctly unpleasant, perhaps even ghastly, although of this he could not be sure, because most of the time it was hidden by the others, appearing on the surface for an instant only now and then.

While he was thinking this over, they reached the inn at Givet. The landlord ran down the steps to offer his shoulder for Mordaunt to lean on as he dismounted; and then turned to show the same attention to his travelling companion, when Mordaunt, who was half way up the steps, was startled by a loud cry almost a scream from the host, and saw him staring at the stranger with his jaw dropped, and every trace of color gone from his ruddy cheeks. The traveller burst into a roar of laughter, and yes! there was something ghastly in his laugh.

When he joined Mordaunt on the steps, to the question, what was the matter with the landlord, his only answer was:

"Oh! Something frightened him."

There was no question about that, for, when he showed them their quarters for the night, he was very uneasy, kept as far from the stranger as possible, and even tried to make the arrangements with Mordaunt, in spite of his almost complete ignorance of French.

Mordaunt now found that his travelling companion had been right in his abuse of the inn, which was small and mean, and so crowded that they would have to sleep in the same room. This, however, was not altogether the fault of the house, as a market had brought such a crowd to the town that they were lucky to get even such quarters.

As they were waiting for their supper by the window, which was open, because the evening was so warm, Mordaunt heard the landlord talking in a most excited way to a group of loiterers in front of the house. He must have told them something very thrilling, as it was followed by an awed hush, broken almost immediately by a babel of excited voices all talking at once. Mordaunt tried his best to make out what they were saying, but his meagre French was swept away by such a tumultuous rush of words, and so he asked his companion what they were talking about.

"Oh!" answered he with a laugh, "the landlord was telling them about the glorious fright I gave him."

What did it mean?

The supper, as was to be expected in France, was much better than the place seemed to promise, and the wine was still better, so they sat over their bottles the whole evening, the stranger keeping Mordaunt amused with his usual flood of lively talk.

When at last bedtime came, Mordaunt, as he rose from his chair, stumbled, and fell with his whole weight on the foot of the stranger.

What was this? This, which gave him such a shock that he had to cling to the table to keep from falling. Could he believe his eyes? But no! It was impossible! It could not be!

Then he began to understand. It was the wine, which was evidently much stronger than it seemed, and had made his eyes deceive him in such an astonishing way. This explanation brought back his mental poise enough for him to stammer out some apology for his clumsiness, which his companion received with high good humor. It had not hurt him in the least, and again he laughed, and Mordaunt wondered how he had ever thought that laugh was jolly.

The fatigue of the journey helped perhaps by his misadventure with the wine, made him sleep like a log till morning, when a noise in the room gave him such a start that he was broad awake in a moment; and then he had to smile at himself, as he saw it was only his travelling companion, who was shaving before a glass at the foot of the bed. But little of his thick, bushy beard was left, and his razor was making short work of that. For a time Mordaunt lay idly gazing at his back, until, catching a glimpse of his face in the glass, with a wild cry he fell back in a dead faint.

Some one dashing water in his face brought him back to himself, and, as he opened his eyes, he found it was his travelling companion, who, as soon as he had recovered, asked:

"What is the matter? Did you see a ghost?"

"Oh! Nothing!" answered Mordaunt, "I have been subject to such attacks ever since I was a boy."

"Next time," said the other, "you will oblige me, if you will have your attack when I am not shaving. Your screech startled me so that I cut this big hole in my cheek."

And Mordaunt, stealing a timorous glance at him, saw a long cut in his cheek, from which a few drops of blood were oozing. It had taken all the courage that was in him to look at that face again, but neither this first timid glance, nor the long stare, which followed, showed the least trace of that resemblance which had just frightened him out of his wits.

But they showed something hardly less terrifying. When he fainted, surely the other had just finished his shaving, and yet now lip, cheeks, and chin were clothed with the bristly stubble of a week's growth.

What did it mean? And what was this thing? He must get away from it now! At once! He sprang from his bed, but, while he hurried on his clothes to escape, his eyes kept straying to it, and every time he looked that beard had grown longer. Yes, distinctly longer, until, when they went down to breakfast—still together—it was the same black bushy growth, which had been there the evening before.

And all the time the stranger's talk flowed on. The same comical, amusing stream—Comical! Amusing! What a mockery those words were! How the jollity jarred on Mordaunt, coming, as it did, from this sinister being, whose real nature was so terribly unlike it!

He followed the terror down to breakfast in moody silence, trying to hammer out some plan for getting away from it. In silence he sat through the meal. For him eating was out of the question, but the stranger attacked his breakfast with the same furious appetite, he had shown the night before.

When at length the horses were brought out, and they were ready to start, moistening his lips, Mordaunt spoke with a great effort:

"We must part here. During the night I have changed my plans. I am not going on with you to Chimay, as we agreed. I must go to Monthermé and Mezières."

The stranger's answer was a loud laugh. What a laugh!

"That's funny," said he, "Do you know, I also have changed my mind overnight, and am going to Monthermé, so I shall not lose the pleasure, the exquisite pleasure of your company."

Although the sneer in this answer was entirely unveiled, it was not insolent enough to give Mordaunt an excuse for a quarrel, so he got sullenly to horse, and they took the road for Monthermé, Mordaunt working over a new plan to shake off this terrible companion, and the other outdoing himself with a torrent of merry stories, each one of which struck on Mordaunt's overwrought feelings like a blow on a broken bone.

The way, running through the gloomy woods and savage hills of the great forest of Ardennes was so lonely that in two hours they had passed but one house, and did not meet a single wayfarer. At length a road, or rather a track leading up through the forest to the right gave Mordaunt the opportunity he had been seeking, as he thought this would in time bring him to the Meuse, when crossing the river he could take the road to Chimay, and escape from this clinging terror.

Accordingly, he pulled up his horse to a dead stop.

"It is time," said he, "we came to an understanding. I shall go no farther with you. You say you are going to Monthermé. Go! There lies the road before you! And I will turn back, and take this cross-road, which will lead me to Chimay and Vervins. Or, if you change your mind again, and decide to go to Chimay, go back that way, and I will keep on to Monthermé, but, whatever happens, I will not ride another step with you."

The other laughed, but, before the echoes of the devilish sound had died away, grew stern and menacing.

"You called me and I came!" he exclaimed. "Now you cannot shake me off. You thief!"

Mordaunt's answer to this was a savage blow in his face.

Horror! His fist struck nothing. It passed clear through that face, as if it were mere empty air.

For an instant he sat thoroughly dazed, staring at his arm, where it passed through the cheek and nose of that thing, and ran a good six inches out behind its head, and it—it laughed that ghastly laugh at his surprise.

Then he fell back, and, as he drew his arm out of the other's head, again he felt no more resistance than from empty air.

As he sat and glared at the man sitting opposite him firm, solid, and distinct in the bright morning sunlight, he knew it was impossible. It could not be that there was no substance, no solidity in this man, who looked and talked like other men. Had he not seen him eat and shave? Had not blood oozed from the cut in his cheek? It must be some trick that made him seem a mere empty show. He would soon punish that cheat!

So crowding his horse up against the other, he threw himself upon him, meaning to push him bodily to the ground, but again in place of firm flesh there was nothing there—nothing whatever—and Mordaunt fell down through the body of the spectre, until brought up by the saddle he lay across its horse with his body passing through its waist. It was a fearful sight to see his head and neck coming out beyond that solid-seeming trunk; but the thing only roared with fiendish laughter, until it had to hold its sides, and, as one hand in reaching for its side struck Mordaunt's head, the solid hand vanished into it without a trace of blow or shock.

With a spasmodic jerk Mordaunt pulled himself up upon his own horse again.

It was true then! There was no substance in that figure.

And then he felt he should go mad, if he could not grasp something, push his fingers against something solid, and he reached out his hand for the other's horseman's cloak, who unclasped it from his neck, and handed it to him saying:

"Oh! You want to feel my cloak."

What a relief it was to Mordaunt to feel the good solid wool! He pinched it. He grasped several of the folds together, and revelled in their substance and their solidity. He rubbed it against his face, and rejoiced in its harsh roughness, until the other said:

"Give me my cloak again!"

And reaching out his hand took it, when, as he touched it, Mordaunt's fingers met through the thick woolen cloth. It still looked solid, but its substance had gone.

This was too much, and setting spurs to his horse, Mordaunt dashed down the road at a headlong gallop. He must escape! He must! He must! But ride, as he would, that feeble limping beast kept just two paces behind, and for all his frantic spurring Mordaunt's powerful horse could not gain an inch.

After this headlong flight and chase had lasted for a good mile, and Mordaunt's horse was beginning to pant with exhaustion, he gave it up, and dropped to a foot pace, his terrible follower still two paces in the rear.

Thus he rode a little way searching desperately for means of escape; and then, as the spectre was going to Monthermé, he determined to retrace his steps, and take the by-path, which ought in time to bring him to Chimay. Accordingly, he turned his horse, and started back over the road he had come. The other also turned and fell in just behind him as before, and thus they rode in silence, until at last Mordaunt with hope once more rising within him turned into the cross-road, when a voice came from behind:

"You have taken the right turning!"

Then he gave up! He dropped the reins upon his horse's neck, and the spectre riding forward took the lead. The road wound up into the very heart of the forest. Narrow and rugged enough at first, as they went on the trees and bushes pressed upon it so that the track could hardly be made out, and they had to force their horses through thick undergrowth, yet still the spectre pushed on, and still Mordaunt followed.

After riding in this way some three miles, they came upon a miserable hut cowering under an overhanging rock; here it halted, and, dismounting, signed to Mordaunt to do the same. Driven by another compelling gesture he tried the door, and finding it fast, threw himself against it with all his strength to break it open, the spectre watching him with grinning mockery, which burst into one of those dreadful laughs, when the strong oak door resisted his utmost efforts. Then passing half through the door it said:

"Step through!"

And Mordaunt stepping through its body at the same time passed through the solid oak, as if it were but air, and found himself inside the hut.

Before he had more than glanced around the squalid, miserable room, unfurnished, unless a pile of musty straw in one corner might be called furniture, the terror followed, and, when it faced him, the thick bushy beard had vanished, its cheeks had lost their florid roundness, the wrinkles had gone from about its eyes, and Mordaunt saw again the face which he had seen in the glass that morning, the face of his cousin, James Bartram. With flashing eyes the thing seemed to tower over him, as it thundered:

"Yes, Henry Mordaunt, it is I! Crouch and grovel before me! You, who cheated me of my father's forgiveness! You, who deceived and robbed your benefactor! You, who altered my father's will, and destroyed me body and soul. But pshaw!" and here his hellish laugh resounded from the crazy walls, as if it would burst them. "I am getting into the heroics, and they are wasted on such a cur as you. Look around! This was my death-bed. Here, after the fever left me too weak to go for help, I lay dying like a rat in a hole, helpless, alone. This was your work. Behold it!"

Then he stretched himself on the straw, and began to toss and turn in the delirium of fever, until the wild light faded from his eyes, the hectic flush died out of his cheeks, leaving them deadly pale, and he fell back in the collapse of complete exhaustion. As he lay thus his cheeks sank into ghastly hollows, his eyes withdrew into the depths of his head, and Mordaunt, crouching against the opposite wall thought it was the end; but soon there came the slightest of motions, and a barely audible whisper:

"Bread! Bread! Only a little piece! Bread! My God! Bread!"

And Mordaunt had to watch all the agony, the gnawing suffering of this death from starvation. Not stretched out over days, but forced and crowded into a few hours, it grew too terrible to bear, and he tried to turn away. He could not turn! His fiercest struggles did not stir his body. At least, then he would shut his eyes, but no! His lids refused to fall.

At last he saw the struggles grow feebler, and, although he could not make out the word, he knew that low sobbing moan was still the cry for bread; and, when with a last convulsive shudder the form in the straw sank into awful stillness, Mordaunt fell forward dead, scattering on all sides the bones of a three year old skeleton.

Lot 13

Every man ought to have a hobby. Mine is old furniture, and nothing gives me quite such a thrill as running down an unusually fine piece and securing it, especially if I can get it for less than was asked, or snatch it out of the mouth of a rival.

I have not had much luck however as, when I was beginning practice, I rarely had money enough to buy the treasures I found, and, now that my work is on the way to filling my pocket, it keeps my nose so closely to the grindstone that I cannot steal time even for the sales, unless they are especially promising.

A little more than a year ago I received the circular of such a very attractive one that I crammed most of my visits into the morning, and so managed to squeeze out time enough for it in the afternoon. But what a mass of rubbish! I walked through the room with my nose in the air, and had fully decided to go before the sale began, when I came upon Lot 13—a tall clock—a perfect beauty shining like a jewel among the worthless old stuff and pretentious modern fakes.

It was the very thing I had dreamed of for a corner of my office, and the more carefully I looked it over, the better I liked it. The outside was all right, and, as one of the auctioneer's men told me the works were warranted in good order, I made up my mind to have it, supposing the bidding did not run too high for me, and I managed to get it too for not much more than I had intended to pay, as most of the usual customers had been frightened away by the rubbish in the other lots.

I left the auction room well satisfied with my bargain, but presently began to have my doubts. It was entirely soul-satisfying there, but how would it look at home, when no longer set off by contrast with those horrors?

Lot 13, too! An unlucky number! How could I have been such a fool? Of course, I should hate it when I saw it at home.

It was well that the crowded visits of the afternoon left me no time to worry over these doubts, for, when I reached home that evening, and found it set up in the corner of my office, I was delighted. It filled the place, as if it had grown there, and seemed even more perfect and attractive than in the auction room, so that I would willingly have paid twice as much.

Its case was simple, almost severe in design, remarkably well proportioned and beautifully finished. It was made of a dark wood, which time had changed to a mellow black sombrely lighted by an underglow of deep red. The whole face was of metal so heavily gilded that the black hands stood out in vivid contrast to it, and the corners outside the dial were entirely covered with a graceful meandering design in low relief.

A broad circle of some white metal ran around the face to carry the black numbers, and inside this the second hand travelled over a little dial of the same sort, while the day of the month was shown through a square hole set in the top of an are of this same metal, on which was inscribed the name of the maker— "Gawen Brown. King Street. Boston."

I was glad it had none of those gimcrack rising moons, or sailing ships, which I have seen on some of these old clocks. They would have seemed impertinent beside its stately beauty.

I put on the pendulum, and hung the weights, and, as the catgut was new and strong, I was encouraged to hope the works were in good order as guaranteed. Then I started the clock, and felt as pleased as a child with a new toy.

As I was putting back the key on its nail inside the case, the clock startled me by a sudden click, as if trying to call my attention to something, but when I looked up at its face I had to smile at myself. It was five minutes before six, and the click was the one it always gave five minutes before it struck.

At the same time this misunderstanding—absurd as it was—did call my attention to something that made me furious—a 13 rudely scrawled in chalk inside the door. This was outrageous! The auctioneer had no right to deface my clock with his marks in this way, especially as I was almost certain that a chalk mark cannot be rubbed off such unpainted wood without leaving a trace. I suppose it was foolish to get excited over a mark inside the door, where it would be seen rarely, but I had fallen so thoroughly in love with my clock that I could not bear to think of a blemish on it anywhere.

My next thought was to wash off the 13, so I got a wet towel and then, as I stooped to the mark it seemed to me odd that it was so nearly at the bottom of the door that to reach it I had to squat, until I was nearly sitting on the floor. Perhaps, after all, it might not be an auctioneer's mark; and, when I looked at it more carefully, I even began to doubt whether it was a 13. It looked more like a B, although a very crooked one, and the more I studied it the nearer it seemed to a B than a 13.

This closer examination of the door showed me that there was writing upon it in several other places, but it was in pencil, and the wood had grown so black that I could make nothing of it in the dark corner, where the clock stood, and must wait till daylight to read it. So I left the chalk mark, until I knew more about it, and went to my dinner.

That evening, as I smoked my pipe in the office, I was struck with the quieting effect of the slow stately ticking of the clock. I had expected to find it rather irritating, before I got used to it, but instead, I found it unusually agreeable from the first. Of course, I may have been prejudiced.

When the next morning gave me light enough to examine the writing on the clock-case, I succeeded in making out near the top of the door

"B. S. 17—"

When I got the writing in a bright light, this was plain enough, but its meaning was very far from plain.

B. S. What could that stand for? I could think of nothing, except brandy and soda. But why should any one record the fact that he had drunk 17 brandy and sodas? And on the inside of a clock-case of all places. It did not seem possible.

Then, too, a man's handwriting was not likely to be steady after 17 drinks, and his was firm and neat. His? But it was not "his"! This was clearly a lady's hand, and that knocked such a hole in my diagnosis that it would no longer hold water.

As I was thinking about it, my eye fell on the figure in chalk—the B, for it certainly was a B, although a very poor one—and it occurred to me that it might have some connection with the B of the B. S. I had just made out. In that case the writing, which came between these two, might hold the key to the puzzle, but, when I looked at this, a cloud passing over the sun cut off so much light that I could make out nothing except the end of one line, which was nearer the edge of the door than the others and so in a better light. This was a 13 in a handwriting not unlike the B. S. 17.

That only made matters worse, for perhaps this 13 had been written there by the auctioneer's stenographer to be copied in chalk afterward. But if that were so, what was the meaning of—

Here the sun broke through the clouds, and in the brighter light I could read without trouble all the writing. I jotted it down on a block, as fast as I made it out, and here it is just as it stood on the door:

>B. S. 17—
>B. S. 15—
>Beatrice Sidmouth 13—
>Beatrice 9—
>Bee 5—
>B 4—
>Beatrice 3—

When I had it all before me on the paper, it did not take long to see what it was. Obviously it was a set of measurements of the heights at different ages of a girl named Beatrice Sidmouth, and the dash, which followed each, was the mark showing how tall she was at that time.

This explanation was undoubtedly the true one, as it explained everything down to the smallest detail. Thus, the lowest mark on the door "Beatrice 3—" was in a female handwriting like that of the highest, but not the same. "B 4—" was the chalk mark already mentioned so often. "Bee 5—" was printed evidently with much labor, and "Beatrice 9—" was in an unformed girlish hand, which had improved in "Beatrice Sidmouth 13—" and became a graceful, delicate handwriting in "B. S. 15—" and "B. S. 17—."

There was something very touching in this record of the growth of a young girl, but reading it gave me an uncomfortable feeling, as if I were intruding on the privacy of family life.

The next evening, while I was indulging in a meditative pipe in my office after a hard day's work, the steady regular ticking of the clock had nearly sent me off into a doze, when it began to behave in the strangest way. For a few minutes it ticked twice, or three times, instead of once in a second, but, when this astonishing behavior had waked me up completely, I found it was ticking with its usual sedate regularity, and decided I must have been dreaming. Just as I was sure of this, it began to run more slowly and kept on falling off, until each tick lasted nearly two seconds, instead of one.

"Curse it!" thought I. "These are the works guaranteed in perfect order!"

When, however, I compared the clock with my watch to see how much these irregularities had put it out, I was surprised to find that it was still exactly right.

What did this mean? Could I have imagined all this crazy ticking? But, as I was too tired to puzzle my brains about it, I sank back in my chair, and closed my eyes for another doze.

This seemed to madden the clock. It gave out an angry bur-r-r, and began ticking with positive fury, so fast and so hard that I heard the pendulum strike against the case on each side.

I jumped up and opened the door of the clock to find out what this meant, but the pendulum was swinging with its usual stately dignity. It was most perplexing! And grew even more so, when after shutting the door and locking it the pendulum had again struck the case two savage blows, before I could get to my chair. I turned back and, opening the door, found it once more swinging just as it should, but, while I was shutting the door again, the pendulum began to move faster, and banged against the case, before I had time to turn the key. This time I opened the door and left it open, when I went back to my seat.

All this was very disquieting. What did it mean? Was I going insane? But I could detect no signs of mental disturbance, even by the most delicate tests, that is, nothing beyond the excitement, which would naturally follow such an astonishing experience.

After I had watched the pendulum—now swinging with its usual beat for some time, I thought I remembered reading about a similar delusion, and went over to my bookcase to look it up. Just as I had convinced myself that it was not in the least like mine, I heard the pendulum hit the case a vicious blow, and, turning, saw it swinging back over a distance twice as great as usual. Then it caught my eye—I was almost going to say—and brought its next swing back to normal with an effort that seemed to rack its works.

After this a few experiments proved that as long as I looked at the pendulum it kept its proper swing, while it began to race the instant I took my eyes off it, so to keep it quiet I sat idly gazing at it for a long time.

Presently I noticed a strange thing. Each time it swung the pendulum seemed to rub off or carry away a little of the wood from the clock case behind it, although it played at least three inches clear of the back. In this way it wore a broad groove along its path, slowly at first, but later so rapidly that in a few minutes it had cut through the back of the case, and after that each swing of the pendulum rolled back the edges of this hole, as it might a curtain, clearing away at first the case of the clock, and later the wall of my office, so that I found myself looking into a strange room, or rather I seemed to be sitting at one end of it.

It was a pleasant room, perhaps a trifle too low, but that made it only the more cosy and homelike. Two large windows faced me, one of them, which was open, protected by a low wooden fence.

Outside I caught a glimpse of a blue sky and bluer sea. But the furniture! It made my mouth water! Such beautiful old pieces plainly heirlooms, which had never known other surroundings. Among them I was not surprised to see my clock standing by the side of the fireplace near my end of the room.

Suddenly a door was flung open, and a very little girl came tearing in. She was screaming with laughter, as I saw, although I could hear nothing except a bubbling murmur that seemed to come from a great distance. Her mother—little more than a girl herself—was close on her heels, and they chased one another in and out among the furniture in a great romp, which grew still wilder, when her young father joined them; until her mother, fairly out of breath, threw herself laughing into a chair, and her father leaned panting against the wall, while the insatiable child stared in wonder that they were willing to stop playing for even an instant, and, when she could not make them begin again, her lip went up, and she crept into her mother's arms for consolation.

Then the man's eyes fell upon the clock, and he whispered something to his wife, who repeated, and explained it to the little girl. At once her eyes sparkled, and she was out of her mother's lap and dancing across the floor to the clock, and, when her father opened the door and got a book and pencil, she jumped up and down in such a rapture of delight, that she could not keep quiet enough to be measured, until her father held her still, while her mother put the book upon her head.

Just as this was at last done successfully, a jangling peal on my doorbell brought me back to real life and my office, but the impression of the scene was so strong upon me that I found it hard to summon presence of mind enough to shut the clock-case, before the patient was shown in.

After he had gone, I spent the rest of the evening in living over again what I had seen. The old-fashioned dresses of the little girl and her mother belonged to a much earlier day, and I suppose an expert in fashions would have known the very year, but I could not place it more nearly than about fifty years ago. I did not dwell long

on this, however, because my mind was more than full of little
Beatrice, who made me think of Landor's Ianthe:

"Your pleasures spring like daisies in the grass
        Cut down and up again as blithe as ever,
From you Ianthe little troubles pass
        Like little ripples in a sunny river."

The next day I tried to puzzle out an explanation of this strange
vision. The most obvious one—that the whole thing was a dream—
I could not accept, because I felt sure I had been awake all the
time, and even if I had fallen asleep, I could not believe that I had
also waked up without knowing it. Besides, a dream would not have
been so coherent and free from anything grotesque or unnatural
except, indeed, the behavior of the clock before the real vision began. No, I could not believe it was a dream!

Later, I remembered that the vision had come to me, while I
was watching the pendulum, and this bright object moving regularly to and fro might well have thrown me into a hypnotic state,
and then the scene would naturally have been suggested to my
imagination, as at that time my mind was full of the measurements
of Beatrice Sidmouth.

At first I was sure this was the real explanation, but, when I
thought it over more carefully, I saw that it did not account for the
strange antics of the clock before I began watching the pendulum.
So in the end I was left without any theory that would explain all
the facts.

One of the things that impressed me the most in the whole affair was the persistency with which the clock forced me to look at
its pendulum, and the almost human ingenuity which it showed in
compelling me to do so.

That evening a more careful examination of the conditions,
which led to the vision, gave me a strong argument in favor of the
hypnotism theory, as I found the electric light was reflected from
the pendulum directly into my eyes, when I sat in the chair I had

used the night before. But I cared much less for finding an explanation of the vision than for seeing, if it would come again, and
was delighted, therefore, when soon after I fixed my eyes upon it,
the pendulum began to roll aside the wall, just as it had done before. This disposed of the dream theory, as now I was certainly
broad awake.

Once more I looked into the pleasant room in the house by the
sea. A few trifling changes in the furniture were not surprising, as
Beatrice when she ran in, was at least a year older than at first. In
one hand she brandished a piece of chalk, and with the other
dragged along her mother, smiling tranquilly at her happy eagerness, while her father followed laughing at her enthusiasm.

The door of the clock was opened and the measuring began.
With what pleased importance she stood still, as the book was ad-
justed to her head! And when she skipped from under it, I could
almost hear her cry: "Let me!" as she marked the line on the door
with her chalk, and then painfully constructed that lopsided B, with
which I was so familiar. When this great work was brought to a
happy end, and her father shut the door, and locked it, I heard the
click of the lock, and the sound, although faint, as if it came from
a distance, was enough to roll back the wall and leave me in my
office alone.

In the course of the evening I tried several times to bring back
the vision, and must have stared at the pendulum for nearly an
hour at a stretch, but with no result, except that it made me very
drowsy.

The next night, however, it was different. In fact, I found myself looking into the same room after even a shorter time than before. The low fence had been taken away from one of the windows,
and both were wide open, showing a broad piazza with an open
railing, through which I caught the gleam of the ocean lying far
below the cliff, on which the house was built. I even thought I could
hear indistinctly the heavy surf pouring in on the rocks at its base.

It was not long before Beatrice came in walking rather sedately
between her father and mother. The measuring was then carried
out with great ceremony, and she laboriously printed "Bee" against

the mark. This was an affair of some time, and required much effort and concentration, the formation of each letter being religiously followed by the movement of the tip of her tongue.

A few minutes later Beatrice sprang from her chair and, running to the door, greeted someone with a great deal of enthusiasm. I expected a child, and was startled to see instead nothing but a small black cloud bobbing into the room, as if it were running. From its shape and size it undoubtedly was a child, and I wondered why I could not see it distinctly, as I did the other people in the vision.

All of them seemed glad that it had come, but I was not, for to me it seemed to throw a gloom over the little party, as if it were passing between us and the sun. After the first greetings it was sent out to play with Beatrice on the piazza. I have no clear idea of what happened next, for the cloud seemed to make everything near it misty, but certainly things were not going well out there, as presently I faintly heard the crying of a child, and saw her mother run out and pick up poor little Beatrice, and while she was trying to console her, her father started to catch the cloud, which scurried out of sight along the piazza. To see better what was happening I sprang to my feet, and at once my office wall closed in on me.

The next night, soon after the vision began, I noticed a strange thing. I had grown into such sympathetic accord with the people in it, that often without hearing a word I could gather the substance of their talk. This was fortunate, as up to this evening I had made out what was happening only by my eyes. I did, to be sure, hear noises in their world now and then, but so indistinctly that my ears were of little use, although each evening I thought I heard more than I had.

After the nine year old Beatrice had written her name on the door with a just pride in the ease with which she did it, my new insight told me that my friends were expecting one of her cousins to pass the birthday with Beatrice, but I thought she did not look forward to it with any pleasure, and I was not surprised when he came, and I knew him at once for the little black cloud of the fifth birthday. It had now taken on the shape and substance of a boy, though even yet it was not entirely distinct, for a mist blurred its outlines, and prevented me from seeing its face, but did not hide its mean and disagreeable nature, and, as on the first time I saw it, I thought it struck all the light out of the birthday party.

It made me hot to see my poor Beatrice exposed to all sorts of teasing and petty tyrannies, until at last, when she was running away from him, he caught her by her braids with such a jerk that she nearly fell flat on her back. When he let her go, she turned and sprang on him with tears of rage running down her flaming cheeks. He was full head taller than she, and I trembled for the result, but I need not have been afraid, for she seized his hair with one hand, and buried the nails of the other in his face with such good will that he flung himself on the ground, and howled like the big coward he was.

Her thirteenth birthday the next evening was not a marked one in any way. She wrote her name in full upon the door; and to my great relief the disagreeable cousin did not turn up, so there was no cloud to mar this peaceful day.

The four years, since I saw her last, had taken away the soft delightful curves of childhood, but I could not regret them with her slender grace and sweet thoughtfulness before my eyes The house, on the other hand, was nearly unchanged, except that the railing of the piazza was now covered by a tangled growth of morning glories in full bloom at this early hour, and I wondered if it would be possible to find a better setting for the delicate charm of my Beatrice.

We were not so fortunate on her fifteenth birthday. The obnoxious cousin was there all day. He was now a student in some college, and had grown into such a monster of freshness and conceit that he snubbed poor Beatrice most unmercifully on every possible and impossible occasion. I could not hear what he said, but my new insight gave me enough idea of it to keep me boiling. My dear little girl, who had nearly rounded into shape in face and figure, bore this infliction with the greatest sweetness, but I could see that it spoiled the day for her, as it did for me.

I saw him a little more plainly than before, although still I could not make out his features. This evening I noticed for the first time the strange gesture with which he tossed back his great mop of hair from his temples with both hands after each of his bullying attacks on Beatrice.

The next evening that I visited the house by the sea the room wore a strange deserted look. All the little ornaments had been put away, and a thin layer of dust had collected on the furniture. My heart sank, as I feared I should see no one, but after I had watched it disconsolately for some minutes, a young woman came in. Could this tall slender girl in the black dress be my Beatrice? As she turned I saw that it was she, and her sad face with the black dress told her story only too well.

She wandered about the room looking affectionately at each piece of furniture, and, when she came to the clock, her eyes filled with tears, and she threw her arms about it and kissed it; then wiping her eyes she opened the door with a sad smile, and measured her height upon it— "B. S 17"—the last of the marks. After that she went to the window, and gazed out over the magnificent sweep of the ocean below. A pathetic figure!

The sound of footsteps made her turn, as her cousin hurried in, and, seizing both her hands welcomed her so heartily that I almost liked him. She was much touched by this affectionate greeting, while he, overcome by her beauty and loneliness, did his best to make himself agreeable. In this he succeeded so well that I began to doubt if he was really the cousin, as his face was completely lost in the mist which still hung about him; but presently he flung his great mop of hair back from his temples with both hands, and I should have known him anywhere by that gesture.

Then they settled down for a long sympathetic talk, and, although I could not hear a word, I felt so like an intruder that I sprang to my feet, and brought the vision to an end.

As "B. S. 17" was the last mark on the clock, I took my seat before it the next evening with some misgivings, for I was afraid I had seen the last of Beatrice Sidmouth. But no! After waiting a few minutes I found myself in the familiar room, which looked as home-like and comfortable as ever, although the cousin sat in the midst of it like a great black blot.

He had grown older and more manly than before, but as far as I could judge through the black mist, which veiled his face and figure, he was still absolutely intolerable.

Presently he sprang from his chair in a fit of angry impatience, and shouted through one of the doors:

"Beatrice! Are you never coming down?" and she called back,

"I am dressing as fast as I can, but I have no one to help me, as all the women are out."

At this he turned angrily away, and strode out upon the piazza in such a fit of passion that he ran into the railing, which broke through before him, and he was within a hair's breadth of plunging headlong over the cliff. He shrank back and for a second or two crouched there quivering with fright. Then, when he had pulled himself together, he examined the railing, and found that the wooden posts rotted away under the mass of morning glories had broken off entirely, so that only the matted tangle of withered stems had held it in place.

Next, a good deal to my surprise, he worked for some time to fit the broken pieces of the railing together again, and had just succeeded in making it look solid as before, when Beatrice came in. Her colored dress showed that several years had passed since I saw her, and they had changed the pensive girl into a beautiful and graceful woman.

She greeted her cousin with no pleasure, did not sit down, or ask him to, and listened most unwillingly to what he had to say. I did not wonder at this, for it was an offer of marriage, which he was pressing, or rather trying to force upon her with even more than his usual overbearing arrogance.

As she shrank from him, I noticed that he was gradually driving her out on the piazza, until she was standing close to the railing, and when, after she had done her best to discourage him, he insisted on an answer, she said:

"No! I tell you. No! You might have taken my answer at first."

On this, muttering: "There is another way!" he sprang at her with a savage push, which threw her staggering against the broken railing. It gave way before her and sent her flying over the cliff. I leaped from my chair to save her, and struck against the dead wall of my office. I could see nothing more, but her piercing shriek, as she fell, rang in my ears. I heard the thud of her body on the rocks below; and then the roar of a higher wave breaking upon them, and through it all his mean, harsh voice in the jubilant cry, "Now it is mine! All mine!"

The callous grasping devil!

Although I had no hope of seeing my dear girl again, I tried many times after this to call up another vision, but without the least result. My clock behaved like any other well-regulated time-piece, and seemed to have given up completely its startling eccentricities.

From the time I first saw Beatrice Sidmouth she had been the greatest interest in my life, but I had not allowed her to interfere with my professional work, which was then at a crucial point, as I was gradually dropping my general practice and becoming a specialist in diseases of the heart.

A month or two after this I was delighted by a letter from one of the larger cities in the Provinces asking me to fix a date for a consultation. The name of my new patient was Endress Whinyard, who was some sort of a judge, and so prominent that I knew him by reputation, although, to be perfectly honest, I have my doubts whether his name would have stuck in my memory, if it had not been such an uncommon one.

When at the appointed time the card of "Mr. Justice Whinyard" was brought to me, I hurried to the reception room with a pleasant thrill of expectation, and found there a thickset man of middle height, whose iron-gray hair had already begun to grow thin.

I gave him a most cordial welcome, but he cut it short in the most arrogant and chilling manner I had ever had the misfortune to meet. So, as he evidently meant to keep the visit on a wholly professional basis, I took him at once to my office for the examination.

When I pushed the door open, and stood aside to let him pass in, the clock greeted us with a loud almost jubilant click—the one it always gives five minutes before it strikes, but when I looked at it, I was startled, for it said twenty minutes before nine—quite fifteen minutes away from any point where it had the right to give that click.

What did it mean?

But I had no time to puzzle it out, for the sound had stopped the judge, as if it had been a bullet. His eyes, almost starting out of his head, were riveted on the clock, and every trace of color had left his face, so that his very lips were ashen. He stood fixed in this way for perhaps two seconds. Then he tottered, and certainly would have fallen, if I had not sprung forward, and caught him in my arms. As I supported him to the patient's chair, and settled him in it, there came from the machinery of the clock a grr like a chuckle of fierce satisfaction.

For some time even the powerful restoratives I gave did not bring him to himself enough to speak, and, when he did at last find his tongue, he whispered:

"There! You see what my attacks are like! Cure them!" Even in this weak state his manner was offensively dictatorial, and I was glad I did not have to appear before him in court.

When the effects of his attack had passed off, he began a long account of his symptoms so rambling and diffuse that I found it hard to keep my attention from wandering, but it came back with a rush, when getting warm in his story he threw up both hands, and brushed the scanty hair away from his temples.

It was he then! That hateful villain!

At first I could hardly keep from springing at his throat, but a little reflection—for which his rambling talk gave ample time—brought me to a saner view of the case. I had no proof he was the murderer, except this single gesture, which for all I knew, might be used by hundreds of others. And even if he were, now that he had put his case in my hands my duty as a physician required me to treat it to the best of my ability.

As I reached this conclusion I began to notice an astonishing change in the ticking of the clock. It had grown louder, more insistent, more masterful, and its speed was increasing very rapidly, until it was running so fast that I could see plainly the movement of the minute hand over the dial.

My glance at the clock over the judge's shoulder made him look round too, and, as his eye fell on it, a spasm shook him from head to foot, and the color once more faded even from his lips. Overcoming my disgust at touching this vile monster, I felt his pulse, and found it racing at 90, which for the moment was nearly as fast as the clock, but only for a moment, as the ticking soon reached at least 120 a minute.

Then it began to go more slowly, and fell off to 90 again, where it lingered for a while, and I noticed that my patient seemed to be bracing himself against an attack; but this tension slackened as the clock fell rapidly to its usual 60 beats a minute, when there burst from its machinery a gurr like the snarl of a tiger that has missed its spring.

For a minute or two the clock hung at 60, and then once more increased its speed, ticking with such fierce insistence that it reverberated from the walls of the chamber, and I seemed to feel it clanging against my brain. As before it soon reached 120, and then growing slower lingered at 90, as if feeling for my patient's pulse, and missing it dropped quickly to 60, where for the second time I heard that hungry snarl from the machinery.

For a third time this was repeated unsuccessfully, but on its fourth attempt the clock, when it came to 90, managed to fall into unison with the beats of the judge's heart, and then, instead of dropping further, it went on with its masterful ticking exactly in time with his pulse.

The judge, who had been fighting fiercely against the terrible assaults of the clock, now completely beaten, sank down in a panic-stricken collapse; and for a time we sat silent, my hand on his pulse, while the walls rang with the overmastering beat of the clock, through and under which I could hear faintly the heavy, satisfied purr of a tiger that had struck its quarry.

Presently there was a change, at first almost too slight to notice, but soon it was plain that the clock and the judge's pulse were beating more slowly. From their excited 90 beats a minute they were coming down toward normal. What did this mean? Certainly nothing could be better for my patient than reducing the dangerous rapidity of his heart. Was the clock then the friend and not the enemy of this sordid murderer? Thoroughly puzzled, I sat for a minute or two with my hand on his pulse, and then light broke on me. The pendulum had dragged his heart far below normal and it was approaching the danger line at 20.

As it was my duty to stop this, I got some nitroglycerine, and gave him a stiff dose, but it had no effect, for, when I felt his pulse again, I was shocked to see how much it had fallen even in this short time.

Next I started to lay him flat on his back, but a warning whirr came from the clock, and I found myself pinned to my chair. My muscles refused to obey me. The clock had taken control of them, as it had of my patient's heart, and all the force of my will could not make them stir me from my chair, or even move my hand away from his pulse. So I sat there powerless to help, while the clock remorselessly ticked more and more slowly, and his pulse followed slavishly.

As I watched his life ebbing away, I was filled with a fierce satisfaction that at last punishment was overtaking the murderer of my Beatrice, and this was echoed by the savage triumphant peal the clock rang out upon its bell, abruptly cut short on the instant its ticking ceased, and his heart stopped dead.

Then both the weights fell to the bottom of the clock-case with a resounding clang, and it has never gone again.

An Undiscovered "Isle in the Far Sea"

Natural history has always been my hobby, so, when my friend, Captain Shaw, invited me to join him in one of his voyages to the Southern Pacific, I was only too glad to accept his invitation, and, although it seemed impossible that my wild expectations could be fulfilled, as a matter of fact the reality even surpassed them. The islands teemed with interest, and the long voyages between were never tedious, since they barely gave me time for the preparation and study of my collections.

At first, however, the trip did not come up to my hopes in one respect, as it was entirely without adventure until a fortnight or so after we had left New Zealand, but then we sighted a small boat in mid-ocean, which was flying, as a signal of distress, a shirt tied by its sleeves to an oar. In it we found three men at the last gasp from thirst and hunger, who told us that nearly a week before their schooner had gone to the bottom, leaving them time to save nothing but their lives.

I was much interested in them, as they seemed to be genuine beach-combers, and fresh from my South Sea novels I set them down as labor-traders, pearl smugglers, or some such picturesque desperadoes. It is possible, of course, that they may have been mere respectable sailors, as they claimed, but in that case their looks certainly belied them.

Soon after this we ran into a fierce storm. I believe we were in no great danger, although it seemed fearful enough to my landsman's eyes, but certainly it was no trifle, as we were obliged to run before it three days; and then after a slight lull it began again even more furiously, so that we could do nothing but lie to for another three. When on the seventh day the sun broke through long enough for an observation, Captain Shaw found that we must have drifted rapidly the whole time that we had been lying to, as we were far out of our course, and in one of the least frequented parts of the South Sea.

Just as he was pointing out to me our position on the chart, before he gave the order to steer for our proper course again, we were startled by a hail from the look out,

"Land dead ahead."

"What!" shouted the Captain, "the damn lubber! Look at that!"

And he swept his finger in a wide circle around our position on the chart. There were no islands within hundreds of miles of us— and yet, when we tumbled up on deck, there right over the bow a faint blue peak was lifting itself on the horizon. I clutched the captain's arm,

"We must find out what it is!"

"Well! Rather!" said he, and reached for his spyglass.

After this we took turns at the telescope, until we were near enough for my field glasses, and then I kept them glued to my eyes. It turned out to be a large island wooded to the top of its central mountain, and unknown—utterly and completely unknown!

I wish I could give you some idea of the thrill—the rapture of such a discovery, but it is no use. It can be realized only by those who have felt it.

We held on until the spouting reefs warned us to come no far- ther, and then sailed around the island keeping as near to the coast as we dared. It seemed to be the earthly paradise, and even now, after the glamour of the discovery has worn off, and, when I am not sick for land after a long voyage, it lives in my memory as the most delightful spot I have ever seen.

The sharp peak, towering from the middle of the island, sloped at its base into a wide plain, falling gently toward the sea. Like the central mountain, much of it was clothed with lofty woods, but else- where it spread into rich savannahs, or smiling valleys carried their little brooks to the ocean. The heavy surf rolled in on long beaches of the whitest sand, or, foamed and roared against abrupt rocky promontories, except on the southwest where it raged at the base of frowning precipitous cliffs.

The blue sea, the white sand, the intense green of the trees against the glory of a tropical sky! What a picture!

Among the trees I made out with my glasses cocoanut palms, orange and breadfruit trees, and many others of species entirely unknown to me. At this I could contain myself no longer.

"We must land, Captain!" I shouted. "We must land! We must!"

But he was not moved in the least. He pointed to the broken line of reefs, which guarded the coast, among which the sea was boiling, throwing up great columns of spray against the rocks, while huge combers betrayed the still more deadly sunken reefs, as they careered over them.

"Too dangerous!" said he. "Do you want me to throw away the ship? I have already taken more risks than I ought."

"Then," I begged, "land me alone! If you won't, I shall swim ashore!"

"Land you alone!"

"Yes! Why not? You can pick me up when you come back. It will not take you much out of your course to touch here, and a fortnight will be little enough for the exploration of the island."

At first he would not hear of it, urging the danger from hostile natives, although, as I pointed out, we had seen no signs of them, or of any other animals, but I was so insistent that at last I wrung from him a reluctant consent, provided I took with me five well-armed sailors.

By this time we had reached our starting point, and, after giving the island a wide enough berth for safety, Captain Shaw called for volunteers, and the whole ship's company came forward. So, as the choice was left to him, he selected five men, three of whom were the superfluous beach-combers.

Now all was bustle. Arms were served out to the men, one of the spare boats got ready and hastily loaded with a tent, provisions, and such other stores as we might need for our fortnight on the island; and in less time than I should have thought possible we were rowing for the land.

A little cove offered some protection from the heavy surf, and here we made a landing, steered through the rollers by one of the beach-combers with a skill born of long experience. As soon as this was accomplished, the Captain dipped his colors in salute, and put the ship about to regain her course.

I leaped ashore, almost before we touched land, and, even while the sailors were pulling up the boat, my attention was caught by some very curious marks in the sand. They looked as if they had been made by thrusting a small tripod into it, and followed each other in such a way that, if they were the tracks of an animal, it was a quadruped, and one with a very long stride.

After the boat had been made snug, the first business was to find a good place for our camp, and we were lucky enough to hit upon a spot about two hundred yards from the beach, which might have been made for our purpose. It was a small plateau, looking toward the sea, bordered on one side by a little stream of delicious water, which afterward flowed noisily down to the ocean.

I ordered the men to pitch the tent here, and, bring up the stores from the boat; and then started with one of them on a preliminary exploration of the country, as I could not restrain my eagerness any longer.

We promised to bring back plenty of fruit for the others, and so were glad to find almost in sight of the camp a grove of trees loaded with unusually large and fine oranges. My first glance at them convinced me they belonged to an entirely new species, because the flowers, instead of having a few stamens as at home, were crammed with them in circle above circle to the number of fifty or more, and, as, too, they had no fragrance, I inferred they relied on the winds for spreading their pollen, and that there were no insects on the island, which later was proved to be the case by a careful search of the whole country.

My study of the flowers was broken off by a furious spluttering and spitting, and turning I saw that the sailor was trying to get rid of a mouthful of dry yellow powder. As soon as he could speak, he poured forth a terrific string of oaths, and after this relief told me that he had bitten into one of the oranges, and it was full of this repulsive yellow powder, as dry as a limekiln and as bitter as gall. We broke open a great many others and in every one of them the pulp and juice had completely given place to this bilious abomination. They were real apples of Sodom.

This was a bitter disappointment in more senses than one, but we were able to bring back a good supply of breadfruit and cocoanuts, and as our mouths were watering for fruit after our long voyage we all set to work opening the cocoanuts. This, however, proved not so easy, for they resisted all our attacks. Even when one was thrown against a rock, it bounced off unhurt, as if made of solid *lignum-vitæ*; and at last, when after a great deal of trouble we succeeded in cutting one in halves with our axe, we found the shell at least two inches thick and the small cavity filled with a green viscid mass, which had such a disgusting putrid smell that no one had the courage to taste it.

There still remained the breadfruit, which we had put on to cook immediately after we got home; but this turned out no better, for it was as tough as sole-leather. We could not get our teeth into it, even after it had broiled the whole afternoon, and, in fact, we found later that no amount of cooking would soften it.

These disappointments threw the men into a very sulky humor. I was not surprised, as all of us had been looking forward to the fruits of the island as the greatest of treats, but they might have taken them a little more cheerfully, and I must confess it made me dread the prospect, if we were to meet with real hardships.

The next morning the beautiful weather and the island laughing in the sun drove away these clouds, which had dimmed our first evening; and after a hearty breakfast we all started off on our first real exploration. Such an excursion after their long confinement on shipboard drove the sailors wild with delight, and I was even wilder, for every step yielded some wonderful discovery.

This is not the place for a detailed account of my observations, which will soon appear in my "Flora and Fauna of the Island." It is enough to say that, although animal life was very scarce, the plants, of which there was a marvellous variety, showed the curious and interesting modifications to be expected in such an isolated habitat.

When, after a most exciting morning, we reached our tent, the first of the men to enter it broke out into such a shout of astonishment that it brought us all up on the run, and there we saw two of the strangest of creatures. The sailor had already levelled his gun at one of them, but I knocked it up and ordered him not to fire for, as they seemed to be entirely fearless, I hoped I might be able to study them alive.

Their bodies of a flattened egg shape about two feet long, one thick and eighteen inches high, were slung from four long thin legs hard and bony like those of a crane or stork. I speak of them as slung, because they were suspended below the knees by the short muscular thighs, which sloped downward at a very sharp angle. This made their knees the tallest parts of the creatures, rising even a few inches above the ridges of their backs, and standing quite five feet above the ground. The body of a mosquito hangs below its knees in much the same fashion.

At eight inches from the ground each leg divided into three still more slender feet, also hard and bony, and ending in a single long massive toe or talon, so that it was evidently the tracks of these animals, which I had observed in the sand on the beach.

Apart from this similarity in general structure the two beasts had little in common. The body of one was covered with a thick glossy black hair, like horse-hair, except that it was coarser, and its head, clothed with the same hair was like that of a huge bird, with a large triangular beak, massive and powerful at its base but tapering to an exceedingly sharp point—apparently a formidable weapon. Its frontal development was uncommonly great and its eyes, which were very large and beautiful, faced to the front instead of being set on the sides of the head as in a bird. Its neck, about two feet long, was thick and flexible, and covered with a black wool. It was usually carried bent, bringing the head against the body so closely that at first I thought the two were attached without any neck. All parts of the beast not clothed with hair were shining black.

The other was much less attractive. Most of its body was bare and of a dirty brownish flesh color; there were, however, a few large shapeless brown blotches irregularly scattered over it, and on these grew a sparse crop of whitish bristles. The head seemed to be a degraded form of the bird-like type appearing in the other. The beak was no longer horny, but soft and flexible, the upper mandible looking like a broad-based pointed nose, while the lower had retreated into a rudimentary chin and a short fleshy jaw armed with two large tusks. The eyes were small and red, the forehead retreating, and, as the back of the head was covered with one of the brown sparsely bristled spots, the whole looked much like the head of a degenerate vicious old man. Its neck, less than a foot long, was bare and not flexible.

The black animal, who had been examining our belongings with great interest, at once turned his attention to us, and looked each one of us over from head to foot with the greatest and most minute care. From time to time he gave out a curious cry— "Ravenole!" which changed to "Graverole!" whenever he looked at the other beast, who, for his part, stood half asleep in a corner of the tent, and seemed as stolid as the other was inquisitive.

We christened the black one Ravenole, and the other Graverole, and to my great satisfaction both of them, instead of being afraid, passed the whole afternoon with us, Ravenole watching everything we did with the greatest interest. He grew especially excited over our dinner and my work in preserving my specimens, and before long had made friends with all of us. Graverole, on the other hand, remained stupid and sulky, or, if much disturbed, uttered a low hiss, except for which he seemed entirely dumb.

When it grew dark, they slipped away, and I spent the evening in making plans for capturing them, if they came back in the morning; but these proved unnecessary, as then they attached themselves to our party, and after that passed every day with us.

Our great excitement on the second day was the exploration of another part of the island, which brought many interesting discoveries, but none striking enough to be described here. I was impressed once more with the extreme paucity of the fauna. The only mammal we observed was a little rodent something between a squirrel and a rat, which lived upon the oranges. We succeeded in shooting one of them, but found its flesh so impregnated with bitterness from its food, that it was entirely inedible.

The effect of the shooting on our two companions was most characteristic. At the report Ravenole started running with almost incredible speed, but pulled up after some ten steps; came back and examined the gun and the dead arboreal rat with his usual curiosity. Graverole only backed into a tree and hissed.

The day's exploration convinced me that we could find nothing to eat upon the island, and this was such a serious matter that the instant I reached home I made an examination of our stores; and found with the greatest alarm they could hold out only nine days, even if we used rigid economy, while Captain Shaw's return was not to be expected in less than fourteen.

I knew that the expedition had been somewhat meagerly provisioned, because we had planned to live in great measure on the fruits of the island, but there was so little food, that I felt certain one or more of the boxes had been left behind in the hurry of leaving the ship.

It was easier to account for our plight than to find a remedy for it, but there was still one hope left. As we landed, I had noticed quantities of a large mollusc at a little distance from the beach, so I called the sailors together, and after impressing upon them the alarming scarcity of our provisions, told them about the shell-fish, and proposed we should collect some of them and see if they were good to eat.

When we reached the shore, one of the men waded into the sea after the shellfish, while the rest busied themselves in launching the boat to get a larger supply of them; but I had no eyes for anything except a most curious network, which covered the whole of the sand left bare by the tide. It was apparently some kind of a jelly-fish, as it was formed of a pinkish-white, semitransparent cord half an inch in diameter, making meshes a little more than an inch across. To examine it more closely I lifted one of the meshes, and thought I must have injured the animal, as it turned deep red on each side of my thumb and finger.

I had just observed this, when a piercing scream from the man in the water brought his messmates to the rescue, but, although they rowed as hard as they could, they reached him only in time to catch him by his shoulders, just as he was sinking. When they pulled him out, I saw, as his legs came above the water, that below the knees they were dangling like a pair of empty stockings. There was nothing left of them but the loose skin. All the solid muscle and bone had disappeared. At first the men were so overwhelmed by this dreadful sight that they could hardly lift the body into the boat, and, as soon as they recovered, they made for the shore at the top of their speed.

I was not less shaken than they, but even this horror was driven out of my mind by the intolerable pain, which now attacked the soles of my feet and my right thumb and forefinger. I staggered to the dry sand, and slumping down there saw that large and deep blisters covered those parts of my hand. Tearing off my boots, whose pressure drove me nearly frantic, I found a similar state of things on my feet. The whole skin of each sole was hanging loose, and a later examination showed that the flesh had been removed from all of these surfaces to the depth of nearly an eighth of an inch.

The position of my injuries seemed to prove that they were caused by the net-shaped jelly-fish I had been examining, and in that case the red stain meant, not that I had injured the animal, but that it had absorbed portions of my solid tissues, after liquefying them, perhaps by the action of some very energetic ferment, which it secreted. If this was true, the beast was also responsible for the fearful death of the sailor, whose bare feet were especially open to its attack. I did not work out this explanation until some days later, for at the time the pain was too intense to allow coherent thought.

The sailors were thrown into a panic by the horrible death of their shipmate, and, as beside two of them had been slightly touched by the beast, nothing would induce them to run the risk of another encounter with it. In fact, it was only by a stern exercise of my authority that I could make them carry me from the beach to the tent, instead of at once putting the greatest possible distance between themselves and the slimy-bottom-beast, as they called this terrible monster, and this they did, as soon as they had laid me on my pallet in the tent. There I passed all that afternoon and night in great agony, so that I was not even able to attend the burial of my fellow victim.

By the next day the pain, although still intense, had subsided enough for me to review our situation, and I realized at once that nothing but the greatest economy could save us from absolute want, as, with the shell-fish cut off, we must depend entirely on our stores, and even on half rations these would barely last till Captain Shaw's return. I explained this to the sailors, and urged in the strongest terms the necessity of using less food, but I might as well have held my tongue, as, so far from coming to half rations, they still went on cooking twice as much as was needed, and throwing away what thy could not eat.

On the second day after my accident, when the sailors were away on a long aimless ramble, and I, worn out by two restless nights, had fallen asleep, I was rudely awakened by a heavy blow on the chest, and looking up saw Graverole straddling across me. Before I had time to take in the situation, he threw out his legs sideways, and once more let his body drop with crushing weight upon my chest. A few more such blows would break it in, and now fully alive to my danger, I grasped him by the throat, before he could scramble to his feet again. The pain in my wounded hand was excruciating, but in spite of it I clung to him, as we rolled over and over, his long legs rattling on the hard earth like drum-sticks.

I soon mastered him, but, as I held him down under me, my chances seemed desperate, for what could my bare hands do against his formidable tusks and powerful legs armed with their three stout sharp talons? And it was a fight to the death, as I could see by the malignant fury, which glared from his little eyes, the maddened gnashing of his jaws, and his fierce hissing—all the more sinister,

because of the weakness of the sound which carried such venomous hatred.

But, as the struggle went on, I took heart, for I began to see
that I was well inside of his long clumsy legs, so that he could not
reach me with his sharp toes, and my clutch on his throat prevented
him from hurting me with his teeth. Indeed, my principal danger
was that the pain in my injured hand would disable me, before I
could strangle him. More than once I felt I could bear it no longer,
but if I slackened my grasp in the least, he renewed the attack with
such insane fury that I was forced to hold on until the end.

When at last I pushed his dead body away from me, I was so
exhausted that I could hardly crawl back to my pallet; and must
have lain there an hour before I had even partially recovered my
balance.

While I was still far from calm, Ravenole came into the tent,
but catching sight of Graverole's body he turned, and began to
scuttle out again. He was an engaging beast, most unlike the malignant Graverole, and I did not want to lose him, so I called him
back in the gentlest tones I could, and, when he paused, told him
the full story of Graverole's attack upon me, for, although he could
not understand the words, I hoped my expression and voice might
reassure him, as he was very intelligent. In this I succeeded beyond my hopes. At first he stood doubtfully in the opening of the
tent, but, as I went on he came nearer and nearer, until squatting
down beside me, he fixed his large beautiful eyes on my face with
the utmost attention. When I had finished, he poured out a perfect
volley of ravenoles with an occasional graverole among them, all
with an air of great satisfaction; and at last stroked my hand with
his beak, which I took to be a declaration of friendship.

After Ravenole had gone, I grew calm enough to realize that I
had gained a priceless specimen, and determined as soon as the
sailors came back to set them to work preserving Graverole's body.
With this in mind I looked gloatingly over to where it lay in the
middle of the tent, and was struck with the change in its appearance. The outlines had bulged out of their original flowing curves,
and in the neighborhood of the stomach the tissues seemed to be

turning into a gelatinous mass. This change, once started, went on so rapidly that after two hours the whole body had become converted into a formless lump of stiff gelatine, like that at one time used for the rollers in printing-presses. Only the legs sticking out of it in all directions remained solid, and they were already sagging, as they lost their stiffness. By the next morning they had grown as thoroughly gelatinous as the rest, and had been absorbed into the shapeless mass. It was a crushing disappointment.

The first day after I was disabled the sailors collected a few specimens for me, but on the second they entirely disregarded my orders, and brought back nothing from their long rambles in the woods; and as time went on, and I was still tied to my pallet by the frightful pain from my injuries, they got more and more out of hand. My helplessness was, I am sure, the principal reason for this, but I doubt if I could have enforced discipline in any case, as the death of our comrade had left only one of Captain Shaw's sailors, on whom we had counted to keep the untrustworthy beachcombers in check, and he had become thoroughly corrupted by them.

It was hard to lie still, and watch their indifference changing into sullen hostility, as the rapid dwindling of our stores forced itself on their notice, although even that did not in the least check their reckless waste.

In time their surliness became so menacing that I began to fear for my life, and I was entirely at their mercy, for, although I kept my revolver strapped about my waist day and night, it was doubtful, if I could use it efficiently with my injured right hand, and at best what chance should I have against four determined ruffians armed with guns and knives? For that matter, if, as I feared, they had made up their minds to get rid of me, they could easily despatch me in my sleep without danger of any resistance from me.

On the seventh day after our landing, while the sailors were as usual wandering about the country, until at noon dinner called them home, I was lying in the tent full of these gloomy thoughts. Whichever way I looked there was no comfort in sight, and I wondered drearily whether I should see another day, and even be allowed the poor consolation of selling my life dearly. Then Ravenole came stalking into the tent, squatted down before me, opened his great beak, and, after a torrent of oaths, said in English—positively in English:

"The sailor-men will kill you."

I was struck dumb with astonishment, and before I could collect myself enough to answer, he swore again profusely, and broke out with:

"Ravenole's the boy! You trust Ravenole! — you! Ravenole will pull you through!"*

What did it mean? Ravenole talking English! It was too incredible! But at this instant we heard the sailors coming back, and springing to his feet he whispered,

"— your soul! You trust Ravenole."

And left the tent.

His confirmation of my fears was fully borne out by the surly fierceness of the men's behavior. They set about preparing dinner, and the last of our stores went into the frying pan without any protest from me, as I saw it would do no good.

As I lay there braced for the attack with my hand close to my revolver, it was some little consolation to feel I had an ally, even if it was only this helpless awkward beast, who, apparently half asleep, was squatting in front of the tent near the rock, against which the men had left their guns.

At last the food was ready, and the sailors were sitting down to it with no sign of bringing any to me, so, as I thought it safer to keep up appearances, I ordered them sharply to give me my dinner. One of them muttered something, that sounded like:

"Don't waste good food."

But another gave him a warning kick, and my share was brought me.

As I ate I kept my eyes fixed on Ravenole and, when the sailors were busy with their meal, I saw him rise cautiously, and begin to pick up their guns from the rock, until he had all four of them

* I represent the oaths by blanks to make his talk a little
   less lurid.

stowed across his beak. That was his plan then, and an astonishingly intelligent one for him, but really how childish and futile!
As, supposing he could get away with the guns, the men could easily despatch me with their knives. And he was not able to carry
through even this simple plan, for suddenly I heard:

"Ravenole!"

The cry was indistinct and muffled, as he was carrying four guns
in his beak, but it was loud enough to reach the ears of the sailors,
one of whom shouted:

"If that straddle-beast isn't running off with our guns!" and,
with a volley of oaths and yells, they sprang to their feet, and
started after him at the top of their speed.

Even yet, however, I did not despair, as Ravenole's clumsy run
was surprisingly fast, and he might get away in spite of the weight
of the guns, but here he lost his head completely, for, instead of
running toward the hills, he turned to the beach, where the sea cut
off his escape. On he ran, the sailors whooping behind, and hem-
ming him in, so that they drove him into the water. Farther and
farther he waded out and they rushed in after him. At last, just as
they were upon him, one of them threw up his arms and screamed.

The slimy-bottom-beast had them.

In a flash it was all over, and the bubbles were rising, where
they had sunk.

Then Ravenole opened his great beak, sending an avalanche of
guns into the sea, and crying exultantly:

"What did I tell you! — you! Ravenole is the boy!" waded ashore
in triumph.

When he joined me in the tent we had a long talk, and I found,
with the greatest surprise that the human intelligence is but a poor
thing beside that of the ravenole. In the six days he had passed
with us, he had not only learned to talk English fluently and even
too idiomatically, but he had gained an idea of the nature of that
entirely strange animal—man, and of his modes of thought and
action, which was astonishingly full and accurate, considering his
restricted chances for observation. This was shown by everything

he said about us, as well as by the ingenious plan he had contrived to get rid of the sailors.

Among other things he told me that he had found out the deadly nature of a gun, when the arboreal rat was shot, and then realized I had saved his life at our first meeting, when I prevented the sailor from firing at him. So, as he learned English, and discovered the men's plot against me, he had hidden his knowledge of the language, that he might protect me the better.

After I had thanked him for this most heartily, and we had congratulated ourselves on the success of his plan, I could not restrain my curiosity any longer, and begged him to tell me about the ravenoles. He was quite ready to do so, and I learned that there were over five hundred of them on the island, but they had withdrawn into the secret recesses of the hills, as they felt a great contempt for these strange animals, which had appeared on their shores. He had distinctly lost caste, because he would associate with us; although he was sure the more advanced among them, if the truth were told, envied him this fascinating study.

The graveroles, he told me, were dying out. At that time there were only seventeen left, and he thought a few years would see the last of them, and, as they were both stupid and vicious, no one would regret their extinction. They were a subject race, but entirely useless; in fact, they could not even feed themselves.

"Why do they become gelatinous after death? I don't know. All I can say is they do always."*

---

* After much thought I have worked out the following hypothesis to explain this strange phenomenon, but I propose it with all possible reserve. May it not be caused by a ferment similar to the one I have assumed in the slimy bottom beast? Although its action must be less intense, as it stops at gelatinization, instead of extending to liquefaction. If there were such a secretion in the body of the graverole, it is fair to suppose that his living tissues would resist it, and, therefore, its effects would appear only after death.

He, naturally, was as curious about mankind, as I about ravenoles, and we became so much interested in our talk, that the long
shadows thrown by the setting sun came as a surprise to both of
us. Ravenole, when he noticed them, sprang to his feet, bade me
good night, and waddled away.

Left alone at first I could think of nothing but my great deliverance from the sailors, and I was filled with joyful thankfulness
and wonder at the cleverness of Ravenole; but this jubilant mood
vanished, as soon as the question of food occurred to me. With
great pain and difficulty I crawled across the tent to our stores,
and found that the few crumbs left in the boxes and the remains of
the men's dinner made barely enough for one scanty meal, so even,
if I could spread this out over two days, there would be nothing left
to keep me till Captain Shaw's return, at the best, five days later.

This threw me into the deepest depression, and in this mood I
began to doubt Ravenole. Might he not conceal the malignant nature of a graverole under a mask of friendliness? Certainly in the
affair of the sailors he had shown himself an adept in concealing
his feelings, and contriving an elaborate plot. Or, even supposing
he meant well, what reason had I for believing he would be willing
to take trouble enough to befriend me? What did I know about
ravenoles anyway?

These dreary thoughts were broken off by the appearance of
Ravenole himself, who stalked solemnly into the tent, opened his
great beak, and poured forth a cataract of shell-fish, one of which
he opened with astonishing skill, and put it into my hand. It was
delicious, and the food problem was solved.

* * * * *

After this the time passed almost too rapidly. In Ravenole I
had the most intelligent and enthusiastic of collectors, and he
showed himself wonderfully expert, too, in preparing and preserving the specimens under my direction, his beak and toes soon becoming more skillful than my rather clumsy left hand.

The intervals of collecting were filled with engrossing talks, for Ravenole was never tired of hearing about our civilization. Often he took in the new ideas with surprising quickness. For instance, he understood the complex doctrine of evolution the instant I explained it to him, and told me there was a tradition that centuries ago the ravenoles had lived upon fruits, and from this he reasoned out at once the gradual extinction of edible fruits on the island, and the development of the peculiar structure of the ravenoles by their struggle for existence against the slimy-bottom-beast.

On the other hand, I found it necessary to begin at the very bottom in explaining to him many things, which seem absolutely simple to us. Thus, it took me many hours to make him understand the nature and uses of writing; and still longer, to prove that it had any advantage over the phenomenal ravenole memory. I did not succeed in doing this, until I had impressed on him the fact that the millions of mankind could be reached only by a device like writing (and printing), while with only five hundred ravenoles there was need of nothing more than the word of mouth.

In return he explained to me the strange sciences originated by the ravenoles, especially their philosophy, so different from ours, but in no way inferior to it in penetration or grasp. This is not the place to give even an idea of it, but when my book on ravenole philosophy comes out, it will introduce to mankind the most startling progress ever made in that branch of study.

Perhaps the strangest thing he described to me was the ravenole language. It consists of but two words "graverole," which means only a graverole and "ravenole," which means everything else, the different meanings being expressed by variations in accent and cadence, but—and this seems almost incredible—in spite of this handicap it is a full rich language capable of expressing as varied and subtle ideas as English. I tried in vain to learn it. Some of the "ravenoles" were distinctly unlike one another, but in other cases my ear was not delicate enough to perceive any difference whatever. For instance, "ravenole," when it meant "shell-fish," and when it meant "evolution through the struggle for existence," sounded exactly alike to me, although Ravenole insisted that the two expressions were as unlike in his language as in English.

While I am talking of language, I may say that, when I had grown intimate enough with him, I called Ravenole's attention to the fact that gentlemen did not swear. He was terribly mortified. Should have noticed that I did not swear, and from that moment I never heard an oath drop from his beak.

* * * * *

When one morning Ravenole brought word that the ship was on the horizon, I found it hard to realize that more than a week had passed. I managed to crawl out of the tent, and together we watched her as she grew larger and larger, until at last she dropped anchor about a gunshot from the shore.

When the boat put off, Ravenole went down to the beach to meet it, but by my advice hid behind a rock, and did not show himself, until he had explained the situation to the landing party, as I could not bear to run the least risk of his being taken for a wild animal, and receiving a bullet.

It was not long before he brought Captain Shaw and his party to the tent. What a delight it was to see them! And with what wonder they listened open-mouthed to my story, although even the most exciting part of it could not draw their eyes away from Ravenole!

When I had satisfied their first curiosity, Ravenole took them for a walk to see the wonders of the island, and then came dinner, when the ship food tasted like real ambrosia after my long diet of shell-fish.

During the meal Captain Shaw and I urged Ravenole to come to America with us, promising him, in addition to the marvels of our civilization, an unheard of triumph in society. We were very eloquent, but he disposed of our arguments by the single question:

"What! To eat salt beef?"

This was out of the question, as the sailors once had persuaded him to try that and ship-bread with disastrous results, and as, of course, it was impossible to take enough fresh shell-fish to last him through the voyage, that plan had to be dropped.

He accepted with delight, however, Captain Shaw's invitation to visit the ship, although first he took the precaution of making the captain promise to return him to the island in safety. I wish I could have gone with him to see his wild enthusiasm, as he poked his beak into everything above and below deck, and astonished all by his interest and intelligent questions.

The next day I was to embark, and at daybreak Ravenole turned up carrying a large bundle wrapped in leaves.

"Here," said he, "is my farewell present. What I know you would like better than anything else—the bones of one of my ancestors. But I hope the other ravenoles will never find out that I have given them to you."

He was right. There was nothing I wanted more; and my present to him—an English dictionary—seemed to please him quite as much.

Then came the parting, and I could hardly bear to say good-bye to this tried friend. As the boat rowed away to the ship, he waved a fore-leg to me from a rock, and shouted:

"Come back in three years, and you will find me the head of a colony of English-speaking ravenoles."

As I lay in the stern of the boat, I kept my eyes fixed upon him, and afterward watched him from the deck of the ship, until he was lost in the distance. Then sadly I allowed the men to carry me to my stateroom. My only consolation was that I should see him again in three years; but I have not been able to go back, as the injuries to my hand and feet have never healed, and the use of them still causes me such violent pain, that my life is passed between my bed and a wheeled chair. I am sorry to say, too, that the trouble in my right hand has delayed very seriously the publication of my great work— "The Flora and Fauna of Ravenole Island."

The Three Nails

When Henry Harding was fourteen, his mother took her family away from the small city, in which he had grown up, to a still smaller manufacturing town, where she had secured work in the mill for herself and her husband—a good workman when sober—and a place in the office for Henry, as she hoped that, after her weak, pleasant husband had been snatched away from his favorite grog-shops and drunken companions, unceasing tactful pressure might give her a chance of keeping him straight.

The plan worked well, but they paid a high price for its success, as the town was a dreary little hole, not much more than a village, and the huge staring cotton mill dwarfed everything, crushing out all beauty and interest with its uncompromising plainness. The boarding-houses stretching out primly on either side were not affected by it to be sure, but only because nothing could make them more unsightly than they were. The enormous factory had blighted even the little river, changing its dancing rapids into a sluggish canal crawling between banks of masonry. The life of the place was as barren as its outer husk, since most of the hands were low class foreigners, with whom the Hardings had nothing in common.

All this was particularly trying for Henry. He hated the neat formal town swept clean of beauty as well as dirt; and his strong natural taste for literature and art had been so cultivated at school that he thought he could not live without pictures and books, and here there were none: No library, no gallery, and no city within reach large enough to have them.

The one bright spot in his cramped and narrow life was Tom McFarland, the son of the principal stockholder of the mill, who in order to avoid paying the salary of an agent was also the managing director. The two boys were about of an age, and the happiest times in Henry's life came when Tom was at home for his vacations from Exeter and later from college, and this although they had little in common. In fact their tastes could hardly have been more unlike, since Tom cared nothing for books, and was perfectly happy if he could have his skating on the millpond in winter and his gun and fishing-rod in summer.

If Henry sometimes felt inclined to grumble that he should not go to college instead of Tom, who thought it nothing but a bore, he kept it to himself, and did not let it interfere with their friendship, which grew more warm and intimate, when, after his graduation, Tom came home to study the business.

Soon after he was twenty-one, Henry was made paymaster of the mill, and, although he was so young, he had fairly earned this promotion by his ability and devotion to his work. This made the Hardings very comfortable, and Henry even began to hope that soon he would be able to spend a little money on books, when his mother's death brought all this to an end, for he promised her on her deathbed that he would take her place, and do his best to drive his father along the rough and narrow path of temperance. Then, after he had taken up his new burden, he could not often make his shiftless father work, and his own salary was barely enough for them to live on. So his days dragged on for two or three more years in the same hopeless monotonous routine—a dreary, stunted exist-ence.

Then came a great piece of luck. One day Tom burst into the office, and shouted, before he was fairly inside the door:

"Hi Harry! Just listen to this! Our selling-agents in Boston have got into a mess about the accounts, and want someone sent down from the mill to help straighten them out. I've asked dad to send you, and he's going to do it!"

Here he executed a triumphant war-dance about the office.

"Think of it, Harry! A week in Boston with all expenses paid!"

Henry could not believe his ears. It was altogether too good to be true, and, after Tom had convinced him that he was really to go to Boston, could hardly wait until the noon bell set him free to run home, and tell his father, but then in the midst of the joyous news he was struck dumb by the horrible thought:

"Had he any right to leave his father for a week?"

The old man noticed his sudden pause of dismay, and understood it.

"No! My dear boy! No!" said he. "Don't feel anxious about leaving me, for I give you my solemn word of honor I will not touch a drop all the time you are away. I should hate to have your well-earned pleasure spoilt by any anxiety about me."

He was so very much in earnest that it seemed impossible not to trust him, and, as he had been behaving very well for a long time, Henry stifled whatever doubts he might feel, and ran upstairs to pack his bag.

The next day saw him established in Boston, where to his great delight he found that his work could be done only in the mornings, and therefore he would have the afternoons entirely to himself; and how he did revel in those afternoons! How he thrilled at the historical sights of Boston, and gloated over the art museum then just budding in the upper story of the Athenaeum!

As for the evenings he made them perfect orgies of reading with the help of a circulating library he had discovered. This was life!

One evening sitting in his bedroom at the Crawford House with the inevitable pitcher of ice-water on the table in front of him he was reading "Midshipman Easy," and, when he came to the adventure with the sharks, it was so familiar that he felt certain he must have read it before, although that could not be, because it was the first time he had succeeded in laying his hands on the book. This was no new feeling with him—probably everyone has had it—but it was astonishing how plainly he recalled every detail of that earlier reading even to the fact that then too he was sitting at a table, and had something to drink before him, although not ice-water he was sure. He could also remember distinctly that this earlier reading seemed not to have been the first, nor for that matter the second, nor even the third time he had read the book, but in each case, what was actually a first reading, had struck him as a rereading, or to speak more accurately the last of a series of rereadings, which gradually faded away in a misty distance. After musing on this for some time he came back to the present, shut up "Midshipman Easy," and went to bed to dream of this strange experience.

When the week of rapture came to an end at last, his father welcomed him home with a blow between the eyes, for the miserable old weakling, in spite of his solemn promise, had sold all their belongings to the last stick, sublet their cottage, and, now that he had drunk them up, was in a most repulsive state of maudlin penitence.

Instead of the pleasant little house Henry had taken such pride in fitting up, they were reduced to a bare attic room in one of the mill boarding-houses, where the scanty furniture was so shabby that it must have been sixth or seventh rather than secondhand. It was really too hard! And his memories of Boston only made this squalor the more intolerable.

One morning a few days later, before it was time to get up, he was lying with his eyes fixed on three nails, which were driven into the wall above his bed. There was nothing out of the way about them. They were common shingle nails, the two on the outside a little more than a foot apart and not quite on a line, while the middle one was some three inches below the two ends and distinctly nearer one than the other. They were absolutely commonplace, and yet they had caught his eye the very first time he came into the room, and since then he spent most of his time staring at them always with an eerie thrill, as if they had some occult influence on his life.

So this morning in the twenty minutes, or so, before he must begin to dress, he lay with his eyes glued upon them, his thoughts meanwhile busy with that ecstatic week in Boston and especially with the strange conviction that he must have read "Midshipman Easy" before. How vivid that was! What could it mean? As he puzzled over this, his eyes were fixed so intently on the three nails that the shabby room faded into blackness.

Then presently he thought he saw two delicate filaments start out of his eyes and uniting a foot away into a single thread, almost as fine as a cobweb, stretch to one of the nails. It was a strange, not over pleasant delusion, and to brush it away he drew his hand across his eyes.

There was something there!

His hand caught on a thread—a real thread—and pulled much more of it out of his eyes!

But how could a thread come from his eyes? It was impossible. And for that matter how could such a slender airy gossamer be so strong. It ought to break at a touch, but a vigorous pull, instead of breaking it, drew out of his eyes another length of it, which lay in a shining loop upon the blanket.

It was too late to examine this queer thing properly now, so he decided to wind it on the three nails, where it would be safe, until he could study it carefully; and, as it still came out of his eyes freely, he kept on winding it, until a good-sized skein was hanging on the wall. At this point he began to feel decidedly chilly, and realized to his great astonishment that he was no longer lying in bed, but standing on a cold floor. Looking around he saw an unknown room, evidently a shop of some kind, as he was leaning against a carpenter's bench close to the three nails, which were driven into the wall at its foot. This was so amazing that he dropped the thread, and turned to find out where he was.

The room was a little one, but its door led into one of those large magnificent bedrooms which he had often wondered at in novels, but had never expected to see. The window, when he ran across to it, looked out on Boston Common, so he knew he must be in one of those fine houses on upper Beacon Street which he had admired so much.

This was most astonishing and confusing, and yet somehow everything was very familiar. He had seen it all before, just as he had read that passage in "Midshipman Easy" before. Why of course that great bed was his, and the sooner he got back into it the better, but, as he turned toward it, he caught his foot in the thread hanging out of his eyes and trailing along the floor after him. That must be wound neatly on the three nails before he went to bed again. So carefully drawing it after him he started for the shop, when at its door a well-filled bookcase brought him up standing, and, as he could never resist books, he stopped to run over at least their titles. One of the first of them was "Midshipman Easy," but then he began to shiver too much to enjoy them longer, and so, hurrying back to the three nails, wound on them what had come out of his eyes, while he was looking about this strange place. A few more turns after this and the two ends of the thread dropped from his eyes leaving the full skein hanging on the nails.

What in the world was he doing here in his old work-shop at this unearthly hour of the morning? Quarter past six! Good Lord! Out of his warm bed without even his dressing-gown! It was very queer! So he scrambled into bed again, and fell asleep, as soon as he got warm.

At eight o'clock he waked up as usual, and, after a leisurely bath and dressing, went downstairs, where his mother welcomed him with a kiss, and, when his father joined them, they all went in to breakfast.

"Well, Harry!" said his father, "picked out that profession yet?"

"No, sir!" said he. "No progress—as usual."

"Oh!" said his mother. "Don't hurry the poor boy! Do let him have a little fun!"

"Fun?" said his father. "Two years of fun seem to me almost enough."

"How can you say so?" said she, "when he needs so much rest after his hard work in college."

His father looked quizzically across the table at Henry, who answered with an amused grin, and the subject was dropped.

After breakfast Mr. Hardinge went down to his bank, and Harry devoted his mind to the important business of deciding how he could get the most enjoyment out of the day. In all this he saw nothing strange, as, when the thread had fallen from his eyes, it had taken with it all consciousness of that other life which he was living in the manufacturing town, and which up to this morning he had thought his only one. Now it was wiped off his mind so completely that he had not the least idea it existed, but believed—as he had always—that he was living only this pleasant comfortable lazy life in Boston.

A month or two later, however, the unceasing round of evening engagements began to bore him, and he was often at his wits' end to find any amusement for the daytime. Then one day, as he was wandering aimlessly about the house looking for something to do, he strayed into the little room next his bedchamber, which had been his workshop, when he was a boy, and there driven into the wall by the carpenter's bench were three nails with a skein of thread hanging on them. It was unlike anything he had ever seen before, finer and more delicate than the finest silk, of a pale yellowish pink color and gleaming with a strange luminous quality.

As he was trying to make out what this curious thing could be, a vague memory grew upon him that it had come out of his eyes, and, when he picked up the loose end, he at once became certain that it had, and began to wonder whether he could put it back into them again. As if in answer to this feeling the end dropped into two strands, which, when he held them to his eyes, were drawn in at once, and continued to vanish into them, as fast as he unwound the skein from the three nails.

At last, when it had all gone, leaving the nails bare, he was kneeling on his bed in the shabby little attic room in the mill boarding-house, and, as it was the end of the noon hour, he hurried away to the office.

Here he had barely settled down to his accounts, when Tom McFarland walked through the room, but took not the least notice of him.

"Hullo Tom!" he called out, "haven't you got a word to throw at a dog?"

McFarland turned with a startled look, and then his face lighted up.

"Why Harry!" said he, "have you waked up at last?"

"Waked up? What do you mean?"

"Well then, have you got out of the mighty queer state you have been in for the last month or two?"

"Queer? How did I show my queerness?"

"You weren't here," said Tom. "That's the only way I can put it. You pegged away at your work just as hard as ever, but that was all. If I spoke to you, I got such a fishy stare that I wondered if you had even heard me, and I could never get a word out of you no matter how hard I tried. I was worried, I can tell you. What was the matter with you anyway?"

"Darned if I know!" said Henry, "but something must have been wrong, for I can't remember much about these last two months. They seem all blurred and indistinct."

They talked for some time about Harry's strange trouble without making any progress toward explaining it, but both were delighted that it had come to an end at last.

That evening, as Harding sat by his stove, he thought over his talk with McFarland, and, after wondering again what had been the matter with him, he tried to recall the last two months, but he could remember them only very indistinctly, as if he were looking at them through a window covered with frost. As he kept his mind fixed on them, however, the frost seemed to melt away giving him larger and plainer glimpses of what lay beyond, until in this way it was gradually borne in on him that his father had died, while he was in this abnormal state.

How could he have forgotten it? How heartless!

But no not heartless, for now that he had come to himself his sorrow for the old man was so great that he forgot all his faults and weakness.

In his next talk with Tom he asked about his father's death, and it was a great relief to hear he had done all that was necessary and proper.

"Although," said Tom, "you did it in a mechanical unfeeling way so entirely unlike yourself that I felt even more worried about you, than I had been."

After this the dreary sordid round of his factory life closed in upon him, and was made even more intolerable by contrast with

Boston, as he had wound back his consciousness of the mill life so loosely that he could see much of that other happier existence through the gaps between the threads.

His only relief from the drudgery was the friendship of Tom McFarland, but what did that amount to, when compared with his love for his mother and father in Boston, or his feeling for the host of more congenial friends he had there.

After a week he could stand it no longer, so he fixed his eyes upon the three nails and his mind as intensely as possible on what he was doing now in Boston. In less than a minute the two strands again came out of his eyes, and united into one, which he wound off upon the nails, till he found himself once more standing by the work-bench in the Beacon St. house.

For some time he stood gazing at the shining thread hanging on the nails, and running his thumb and forefinger abstractedly over its smooth pleasant surface. As he did so, he became vaguely conscious of that other life he was leading in the distant mill town, but it was all very remote and misty. He was certain, however, that he had made the passage from that first life into this second one by winding the thread out of his eyes, and that he had done this, because, when he read "Midshipman Easy," he remembered reading it before—in this second life of course. Yes! He had read it in his sophomore year, and, when he came to the episode of the sharks, he had been sitting at his table with a mug of beer in front of him. Then it came over him with a strange thrill that during that reading he knew he had read that passage before in some other existence, and it had not been his first, his second, nor even his third reading of it.

Why this could only mean that he was leading several other lives! What were they like? He wondered.

Perhaps he could wind off the consciousness of this Boston life, and pass into his third existence. It was worth trying at any rate. So he fixed his eyes on the three nails and his thoughts on the passage in "Midshipman Easy," of which he had such a multiple remembrance, and sure enough presently another thread came out of his eyes, and he wound it on the nails outside of the skein already hanging there.

As he went on winding, a close fetid stench nearly choked him, and then his arm began to grow stiff, and grinding pains shot through all his joints. When at last the end of the thread dropped from his eyes, he was lying on some mouldy hay, which barely raised him above the dank earthen floor of a filthy cellar. On all sides lay revolting paupers—covered with sores and vermin, and the single dirt-encrusted window shut out all wholesome air, and let in scarcely any light.

Where was he? He had been puzzling over that question ever since he was brought here some days ago. He could remember leaving Rustchuk, but after that his memory was very misty, when it was not a complete blank.

He had certainly been attacked by robbers. He could never forget that fearful night, after they had stript and left him. Ugh! How cold it was! Or the long agony of that jolting ride on the donkey, which had landed him in this hell.

But where was it?—He had not the least idea, and he could not ask, since the language with much else had been knocked completely out of his head.

What a damnable idiot he had been to try to work up that set of magazine articles! And yet they must have taken with such a title— "Rambles in Roumelia and Roumania." Well! It was all up now! Here he was with a broken arm and this cursed rheumatism, and not a cent to his name! The notes for his articles gone too! Good Lord!

Then he noticed the end of the thread, which was still in his hand, and glanced up at the skein hanging on the three nails driven into the wall above his lair. That, he remembered, had come out of his eyes, and linked him to another life. Why not go back to that other life? It could not be worse than this.

But, if he was going back, he must do it quickly, for, as the rheumatism tightened its grip upon him, his one remaining arm was stiffening, and would soon grow useless. With trembling fingers he lifted the thread, and, as it split in two, held the ends to his eyes. They were sucked in at once, and then he began to unwind the skein with such slow clumsy fingers that he feared he was too late after all; and yet in spite of this anxiety he forced himself to wind the consciousness back, as tightly as he could, so as to cut off any possible connexion with this revolting life.

What a relief it was, when at last the skein was all back in his eyes, and he found himself once more in his happy Boston life! Without the slightest wish now to find out what his fourth and fifth lives might be, for even the very quintessence of bliss could not tempt him to pass again through the barrier of that devilish third life.

After this his Beacon St. life flowed on peacefully and happily with no incident worth the telling, until, when at last he felt ashamed to postpone any longer the real business of his life, he happened to meet a friend named Ripley (a junior partner in one of the large selling houses), who asked him, if he had ever thought of taking up manufacturing.

"There is," said he, "an excellent chance just now in one of our cotton-mills, which needs more capital to enlarge its works, and I am sure would jump at the chance of taking you in, if you bring them this capital. I am going up to the mill tomorrow on business. Why not come along, and spy out the land?" This seemed too good an opening to neglect, so the next morning found them in the train.

A long tedious journey brought them to an ugly little town cowering below a many-windowed monster, and there in the office of the mill they found Mr. McFarland, the principal owner and manager, a lean, tall old man, who received them with an air of bored superiority, and hurried through the business that had brought them. When, after it was finished, Ripley said his friend would like to see the mill, McFarland turned back to his desk calling over his shoulder:

"Henry!"

This brought an insignificant little man in from the outer office, and, after McFarland had said without even looking up: "Take these gentlemen over the mill," he seemed to forget their existence.

Hardinge followed the young man fuming. He was not used to being treated in this way, and the visit to the factory did nothing to give him a more agreeable impression. There might have been a poorer guide, but it is doubtful. He seemed half asleep, volunteered nothing, met questions with an uncomprehending stare, and, if pressed for an answer, gave the smallest amount of information possible in the fewest words. In spite of all this, however, Ripley seemed to enjoy trying to draw him out, until seeing how furious Hardinge was growing, he cut their visit short, and at the door of the mill they left their guide in the same vacant daze, apparently hardly conscious that they had gone.

Then Hardinge burst out: "What a damned conceited ass!"

"Oh!" said Ripley, "why don't you take McFarland as a joke? I do."

"A joke! That old ass! You've got a queer idea of a joke."

"Old McFarland *is* an ass," said Ripley, "but he is not such a bad old boy after all. The trouble with him is he has always been so much the biggest toad in such a very small puddle."

"I don't want anything to do with him, or his damned puddle," said Hardinge.

"Well anyway," answered Ripley, "you must have enjoyed seeing him chuck away his best chance of getting that new capital he needs so badly. It will be fun to see his face, when I tell him what he has done."

Hardinge merely grunted: "Let's get out of this."

"But," said Ripley, "didn't that clerk, who took us through the mill, make up for everything? I would have gone twice as far to see him."

"Why? What the devil was there about him?"

"He was so exactly like you."

"Like me? That little runt! Like me! O—" Here he choked with rage.

"That was just the queer thing about it. He did not look like you. He did not talk like you. He was a good head shorter. There was nothing about him that was like you, and yet he was you. I felt I was speaking to you every time I spoke to him, and it gave me a queer uncanny feeling to have two of you with me at once."

"Thank you for the compliment!"

"There's nothing to get huffy about. Didn't I tell you he was not the least like you? He was you! That was all."

This experience disgusted Hardinge thoroughly with manufacturing, and, just as he began to think of being a banker, all his plans were set aside for a time by a trip to Europe with his father and mother.

For more than a year they wandered over the Continent, toward the end of the time with another family of pleasant Bostonians, and as these friends had a charming young daughter, it was not strange that the engagement came out, before they sailed for home. The match was most desirable in every respect, so after some months of unmixed bliss— the greatest thing in life for the young people, but the dullest for everyone else—the time for the marriage was fixed, and preparations began in earnest.

With his usual method and energy Hardinge finished all his own preparations so promptly that he found himself on the day before the wedding with nothing to occupy his time. The bride of course was too busy to be seen, and he was altogether too restless and nervous for reading, or any of his usual occupations.

The day dragged along, as if it would never come to an end, and, when that evening he realized there were twenty-four hours more of this sort of thing, his heart sank within him. How could he ever get through them? Then it happened he went into his old workshop, and there saw the three nails with the skein of glistening thread hanging upon them. Had not this something to do with another life? And then, as he touched the thread, the whole connection between this life and the one at the mill flashed into his mind and with it a bright idea.

Why not wind himself back into his mill life, until the time of the wedding?

In that way he would get rid of the intolerable boredom of these endless twenty-four hours. He did not need to think twice about it, but began at once putting the thread back into his eyes, taking pains, however, to wind it so loosely that he would have a very fair idea of what he was doing in his Boston life.

Next morning, while he was dressing for the mill, this double consciousness made him grin at the horror his Boston self would feel, if compelled to get up at such an hour; and, when he reached the office, although his other self recoiled from the mechanical routine, he felt it was better than that deadly waiting in Boston, or, if it was not, whenever he wished, the three nails would take him back to his second life.

Early in the day Tom McFarland walked through the office, paying no more attention to Henry, than if he had been a chair, but when he called out:

"Good morning, Tom!"

McFarland started, as if he had been struck, and, alter he had taken in the truth, shouted:

"What! Harry! Are you really here again after all these months?"

Then seized his hand and nearly shook it off. From the talk that followed Henry was not surprised to find that he had been in that strange absent state for over a year. As for Tom he was bubbling over with delight, but at last tore himself away, because, he said, he had some pressing business that could not be put off.

All through the morning he kept flying in and out of the office, and in the last ten minutes before the noon hour, ran in at least three times to ask Henry, if he was not almost ready to go home. Henry himself was quite as impatient to get to his room, since he was going to wind himself back into his Boston life, as soon as he reached it. What if there were still eight hours before the wedding, surely he could manage to worry through them with the help of his dressing and other preparations, and it was safer to be on the spot.

When at last the noon bell rang, and he was changing from his office to his street coat, Tom bounded in again, and said he was going home with him. Henry wished him in Jericho, but after all it made no real difference, Tom could not stay more than half an hour at the worst, and he had loads of time.

At the boarding-house Tom ran up the stairs first, and, as Henry reached the top, called out,

"There! Old man! Look at this! Here's a surprise I've got up to celebrate your coming-back."

He threw open the door.

The room had been repapered! The three nails were gone!

It was a terrible blow!

For a minute or more Harding could not get out a word, but Tom did not notice it, as he was walking about the room admiring the paper and his taste in choosing it, and almost as much the quickness of the paper-hanger, who had managed to get the job done in a single morning. This gave Henry time to remember that he could get back to Boston and his wedding by simply driving in the three nails again, so that he was able to seem properly grateful for this well-meant kindness, but he was on pins, until Tom went.

Almost before he was out of the building, Henry ran down to the store, and bought a hammer and a package of shingle-nails. Then back to his room, drove three of the nails into the wall above his bed, and saying to himself:

"Now I shall be in Boston in a few minutes," lay down, fixed his eyes on them, and thought with the greatest intensity about what he was doing in Boston.

A minute passed—two—three—long minutes. Nothing happened.

He struggled even more desperately to draw the thread of consciousness out of his eyes, but there was not the least sign of it.

Could it be that the nails acted only when in exactly the right position?

He studied them carefully.

Yes! He was sure they were somewhat too far apart. He corrected this, but still no thread.

Then he saw he had driven in the two end ones on the same level. How stupid! He lowered the furthest one—no result. After several experiments in this line, he began working on the middle nail, changing its position a trifle, now this way—now that—now up—now down, but still nothing. Nothing!

Then a fearful doubt grew on him.

Could he get back at all?

That must be settled at once, and he began to work even more feverishly, until, after he had used up the whole of the dinner hour, he was obliged to go back to the mill no nearer Boston than when he started.

How glad he was now that he had wound his mill-consciousness back loosely enough to get frequent glimpses of his second life through the gaps between the threads! In this way all through that long wretched afternoon he was aware that he was trying, not over successfully, to kill time in Beacon Street.

Oh! If only he were there really! What was any amount of boredom to the crushing fear that he might not get to his wedding at all?

When at last the mill shut down, he rushed home to try an idea, which had occurred to him in the course of the afternoon. It was to scrape off the paper, find the original holes, and put the new nails into them; but it was easier to decide to scrape off the paper than to do it. It clung to the plaster with a tightness little short of devilish; and, after he had succeeded in uncovering that part of the wall, he found he had made so many new nail- holes that he could not find the old ones, in fact there was a yawning gap over an inch wide, where the middle nail should have been. This forced him to go back to his first plan of driving nail after nail, until chance led him to the exact arrangement, which alone would attract his consciousness.

He must hurry too! There was not over-much time left, for he had laid out his wedding clothes some time ago, and now, when in trying three of his nails he fixed his mind on that other life, he was already putting them on.

Of course it was ridiculously early to begin dressing, but it meant there were still only two hours, and, if he did not get these plaguey nails right, he should miss the wedding. Actually lose his own wedding! No wonder his hammering grew fast and frantic, and that he grudged even the few minutes needed to buy a second paper of nails. He must get free from this beastly hole in time

Now he was dressed and going down to his carriage.

Now driving to the church.

There was no use going on any longer. It was too late!

Down he skimped in a heap upon his bed and fixed his whole mind on the ceremony.

His wedding! And he was not there!

Was there ever such a maddening situation! A mere spectator at his own wedding! And from a distance of more than one hundred miles too!

As soon as it was over, and he was driving away from the church with his bride, he flew back to his feverish hammering, sure that at last he must succeed after so many trials. But no! No better luck! So he could only watch from afar dimly his own wedding reception and his start on the honeymoon, and then, completely worn out with excitement and want of food, he threw himself on his bed, and for a time lost his troubles in uneasy sleep.

The next morning almost before daylight he was out of bed and his hammer was going again; and so day after day he went on, always hammering, but achieving nothing except noise; until the other lodgers protested, and he was able to work only in the few hours of daytime he could snatch from the office.

One evening a week or so later he ran round to Tom McFarland's house, and, as soon as he could catch his breath, gasped out:

"You must come with me to my room, for we have been good friends, and you ought to see the last of me."

"What is the matter with him?" thought Tom. "Does he mean to kill himself? He is excited enough to try it, but I have got my eye on him." And he hurried on by Henry's side ready for anything.

When they reached the room, however, his first look at it drove everything else out of Tom's head. Its walls bristled with a thicket of nails—hundreds of them—driven without any apparent plan, or regularly all over the paper he had taken such pains to select, and, as if that were not bad enough, in one place a great patch of it had been scraped off the wall.

While he was glaring at this too angry to speak, Henry came up to him with a strange light in his eyes and slapping him on the back said:

"Well Tom! I wish it were not goodbye! I shall miss you terribly, and never forget how kind you have been to me."

Tom looked savagely round at the ruined wallpaper.

"This does not look like it I know," he went on, "but you would not mind, if you knew all. And now it is really Goodbye, for I am going to cut the skein."

He held out his hand to Tom, who would not even look at it.

"After all," said he, "no matter, as this is the end of me."

Tom, furious as he was, braced himself to spring on Henry and hold him, if he tried to do himself a mischief, but there were no signs of anything of that sort. He was only standing quietly look-ing at three of the nails and seemed to be falling into a trance.

Then, as Tom saw there was no danger, his anger flared up again, and he began to tell Harding what he thought of him, when the words died upon his lips from sheer amazement, since he saw, or at any rate thought he saw, stretching from Henry's eyes to the nails a delicate thread, which he wound off upon them, until a gleaming skein was hanging there. While McFarland stared at it, wondering if his eyes were not playing him false, the skein parted, as if cut in the middle, and the two pieces hung swaying from the end nails.

"What the devil does this mean?" he asked.

But Harding turned on him two vacant glassy eyes, from which the man himself had vanished—and since then he has never come back.

A Remarkable Case

Every year, when the summer comes again, I congratulate myself that I am not one of those physicians, who are tied to the city by their practice, and wonder how those poor devils manage to worry through the year without a long vacation. Then I thank Heaven that I have money enough to devote my life to the science of medicine instead of the art, for beside being the career I like, it does not stand in the way of long vacations. In my first enthusiasm, to be sure, I jeered at the idea of wasting a whole summer in doing nothing, but now experience has shown me that with three months' rest and change in the hot weather I do better work and for that matter much more of it, than if I kept my nose always against the grindstone.

A few years ago I passed July and August in a New England farmhouse with an especially jolly party. There were picnics once or twice a week, so that by the beginning of September we had seen all the attractive places in the immediate neighborhood, and decided to conquer a new world by spending a day at Pickerel Pond—a drive of more than eight miles.

As the only barge in our village was not large enough to hold all of us comfortably, we agreed that I should drive my Cousin Juliana to the pond in my buggy. When the day arrived, we gave the party in the barge a good long start, and yet in spite of that we caught up with them after a few miles, and drove past at a brisk trot paying no attention whatever to their shouts of, "*Where* are you going? How are you going to find the way? Drop in behind us, if you want to see Pickerel Pond. Plenty of room behind!" and so on, but I did not intend to swallow their dust, and so drove on bravely, although I had never been to the pond, and had only rather vague ideas about the road.

At first I felt sure I had hit it, but about quarter of an hour after we had left the barge out of sight, I began to have my doubts, and a few more confusing turns changed them into the certainty that we were lost; I kept on somewhat further however, as I did not relish the idea of driving back ignominiously and following the barge—that is supposing we could find it, of which I was by no means certain. Then, just as I had given up all hope, we came upon a set of bars in the middle of a stone wall with a faintly marked track leading across the field to a patch of woods beyond. So we had hit it right after all, for this was the entrance to Pickerel Pond, if I could trust the description of it.

Giving the reins to Juliana I got out, took down the bars, and we drove through leaving them down for the barge.

When we got through the narrow belt of woods, the road ended not at a pond but before a house shut in by a picket fence so high and strong that it looked more like a stockade than a fence. It was not Pickerel Pond then after all, and, when I started for the house to ask the way, I found a young man just inside the gate, who seemed very much confused and embarrassed by my question:

"Can you tell me the way to Pickerel Pond?"

But he quickly pulled himself together and answered:

"Pickerel Pond?—Pickerel Pond! O yes! This way. I'm the man to show you!"

So I fastened my horse with the weight, helped Juliana out of the buggy, and we followed the young man, who led the way around the house with an air of the most exaggerated ceremony, as if he were an usher at some great function of state. Sometimes he would strut on before with a pompous stride, and then pausing wave us on with the magnificent gesture of a Lord Chamberlain. His behaviour was so absurd that I thought he was making fun of us, but, when he saw I was taking offence, he seemed utterly abashed, dropped his ridiculous manners, and slouched along in front of us muttering:

"Pickerel Pond! Pickerel Pond!" over and over again, faster and louder at each repetition, until his voice rose to a scream, when he seemed to remember our presence, and fell to muttering again under his breath. It was perfectly clear now that he was out of his head, and, while I was wondering how we could get away from him, we reached the back of the house, where there was another gate leading out of the enclosure. As he started to open this for us, I noticed that it was secured in a most curious way by a long bolt toothed on its lower edge, and moved by turning the handle on a cog-wheel, which played into these teeth. This shot the bolt so slowly that it would take him at least five minutes to open the gate, and all the time he kept chattering:

"Pickerel Pond! Pickerel Pond! He can! He can! Yes! Yes! He can! Hoo! Pickerels! Ponds of pickerels! Pickerel Ponds! He can! He can!" until, as his excitement grew, the words changed into piercing shrieks, and I saw he was a violent, perhaps even a danger-ous, lunatic, and we must get away at once. So I thanked him for his trouble, and telling him quietly and politely that we had de-cided not to go to Pickerel Pond took Juliana's arm, and turned toward the buggy.

While I was speaking, he glared at me stupidly, but, as soon as we started to walk back, he became outrageous again whirling and springing about us, brandishing his arms in the air, and pouring forth volley after volley of the maddest ravings.

I was now thoroughly frightened, and hurried Juliana along as fast as I could go without seeming to run away, until we came in sight of the front gate, when I whispered to her:

"Run out to the buggy! Undo the weight, and climb in, while I hold him off."

Then, when we were nearly at the gate, I turned and faced him with as much calmness as I could muster. This brought him to a standstill for the second or two Juliana needed to slip through the gate, but, when walking backward and keeping my eye fixed upon him, I also reached it, he suddenly leaped forward and would have got to it before me, if I had not caught him, and with a vigorous push thrown him to his knees several feet away. Before he could get up, I was outside the gate, and had slammed it behind me, while he crouched there looking more like a mad dog than a human being.

Then staggering to his feet he rushed at me in such a frothing fury that I was thankful the gate was between us. The next minute he was shaking it, and gibbering, and yelling at me through it. I was safe for the moment, but the situation was desperate, for how could I get a long enough start on him to run to the buggy, and climb into it.

Suddenly a shriek from Juliana made me look around, and there between her and the buggy was the maniac! There outside! But it could not be, for I saw him here inside. Yes and felt him too, as just then he stooped, and bit my hand which was holding the gate.

I must have dreamed he was attacking Juliana.

No! He was there too! He was there too capering and scream-ing around her body, as she had fallen in a dead faint!

Whatever happened he must not hurt her, so I dropped the gate, and ran to help her, but, before I had taken two steps, he blocked the path in front of me. A third!—Not one of the other two, for over his shoulder I could see one of them raving beside Juliana, and the noise at the gate told me the first was there too.

He was there! And here! And here! He was everywhere! For now on my left I saw him coming again, and a howl from my right showed me another rushing down on me there, and then more and still more came trooping in on me from all sides.

Thoroughly unnerved I fell to the ground, when all of them joined hands and danced around me in a ring with deafening yells.

I drove my face into the grass to shut out this hideous night-mare. What next? What next?

Then I heard a quiet voice say:

"Eight! I never saw so many before."

And sitting up I saw the ring of screeching devils had vanished, the young man was walking sheepishly toward the house, and a young lady with a sad quiet face was coming down the road.

I stumbled to my feet too much shaken even to feel embarrassed at my ridiculous position; and then, as she looked at me, her face lighted up, she quickened her pace, and came up to me smiling and holding out her hand.

"Why Dr. Steele! Don't you remember me—Miss Nesmith?"

Now I recognized her. Some three years before I had known her fairly well, but since then had lost sight of her completely. I saw many new lines of care and anxiety upon her face, but with them a firm and noble courage, which brought me back at once to the world of sanity and common sense. What a relief it was to escape from that crazy nightmare!

Her next words too were reassuring.

"You need not be afraid. He will be perfectly quiet after such a bad attack, and at any rate you will not see him again.—Oh poor thing!"

This last as she caught sight of Juliana. We picked her up and carried her into the house, where it was not hard to bring her to herself again; and, after she needed nothing except a quiet rest before undertaking the ride home, we went into another room, where Miss Nesmith turning to me with pathetic earnestness said:

"I feel as if Heaven had sent you to help me, and I *do* need help! I need it terribly! You have seen his doubles. You know there are such things. Will you help me?"

This appeal swept me off my feet, and I told her I would do anything I could to help her, but she cut me short.

"No! no!" she burst out. "I do not want an answer now. It is no small thing I am asking. It is a great sacrifice, and you must hear everything and think it over carefully before you decide."

This fine restraint in spite of her terrible need touched me even more deeply, and again I began to promise her my help, but again she refused to listen to me, until I had heard their story.

"Our troubles," she told me, "began three years ago, when we took a house at Swampscott for the summer. One day my brother swam out far beyond the other bathers, as he did very often, and became entangled in the feelers of a poisonous jelly-fish. He was completely paralyzed, and would have been drowned, if there had not been a boat near enough to save him.

"The paralysis went off entirely after a few days, but the shock to his system did not, and from a cheerful, active young man it changed him into a depressed invalid, who would sit in sullen brooding for hours, or burst out into fits of excitement, which frightened me even more.

"I hoped time would cure him, but instead he grew worse, until his talk began to be wandering and incoherent. I would have given anything for the advice of a doctor, but he would not hear of calling one in, and, if I suggested it, he broke out into one of his terrible attacks of excitement.

"One day a month or so after his accident he asked me how much I thought a *saké*-cup would hold. I laughingly told him I had not the least idea, and, when I asked him why he wanted to know, he grew so violent that I changed the subject as soon as I could.

"The next day he was so alarmingly sick that without consulting him I sent for the doctor, who pronounced it a case of poisoning with a number of different drugs, and told him he would have serious trouble, if he tried such an experiment on himself again. He listened in moody silence, and, as I saw the visit was goading him to fury, I brought it to an end as quickly as possible.

"After the doctor had gone, I wondered why a *saké*-cup sounded so familiar to me, and then remembered it had been mentioned in a book of Japanese stories, we were reading the last thing before his accident, in fact, as we started for the beach, we had just finished an amusing account of an odd sickness called the soul-dividing disease, which caused a man to throw off a double exactly like himself except that it could not speak. The cure for it was a *saké*-cup full of several very unpleasant medicines. I felt certain this story had suggested the *saké*-cup to his mind, but could not make out why he should have taken the medicines, supposing they were the cause of his attack.

"Then I forgot all about it in my anxiety for him, until a day or two later it was recalled to my mind in the most shocking way, for then, I saw one!

"Something had excited him more than usual, and he threw off a double.

"How frightened I was, when the dreadful thing came skipping at me in a sort of crazy dance! I nearly fainted, but dared not give way for fear of what might happen to my brother, if I did. After a hard struggle I managed to get enough control over myself to speak to him firmly and calmly, and the hateful double vanished.

"Some days later he threw off one again, and, as I was at my wits' end to know what I ought to do, I consulted the doctor, but, before I had half told him about the case, I saw that he thought it was not my brother who was insane; so I broke off in the middle of my story, and hurried away from his office terribly afraid that he might act on his suspicions, and have me shut up, and then what would become of my poor brother?

"For the rest of that day and the sleepless night that followed I did nothing but make and reject plans, until at last I decided there was but one way out of our troubles; and the next day I packed up our things, paid off the servants, and left Swampscott with my brother on the first afternoon train.

"I then had this house built and by a free use of money succeeded in getting it finished in two months, but these two months were a perfect nightmare to me, and I did not breathe freely, until we were settled here in this out of the way place, and safe from any attempt to part us.

"Even in this quiet and secluded life he did not improve, but threw off a double every time that he became excited; and it was impossible for me to guard against these attacks of excitement, as frequently they came without any apparent cause.

"After some months his disease took a new turn and a very startling one, for he threw off two doubles instead of one during a more violent fit than usual, and for the better part of a year afterward he always threw off two, when he was especially excited. Then the number rose to three; and after this became one more at intervals of about six months, until just before you came it had grown to seven, and the fierce excitement from your visit brought it up to eight."

After Miss Nesmith had come to the end of her story, she leaned toward me, and said:

"Now that you know all, will you take the case? That is, will you come and live here for a time, and see if you can do anything for my poor brother? It is a great thing I am asking, but my need is great."

My answer was, "When shall I come?"

But she said:

"No! I cannot accept your generous offer now. Wait till you have had time to think it over carefully, and then, if you have not changed your mind, I shall be most grateful to you; but, if you find you ought not to do it, I shall understand, and not blame you in the least."

"You will see me tomorrow," I answered.

As by this time Juliana had taken a long enough rest, we bade Miss Nesmith good-bye, and drove home. On the way I managed to persuade her that instead of really seeing the doubles, she had imagined, or dreamed them, when she fainted, after the crazy man had chased her. So she begged me to say nothing about her "silliness," as she called it, and, when I of course agreed most willingly, we decided to tell the others that losing our way to the Pond we had happened on an old friend of mine, and passed the afternoon with her.

Juliana went to bed, as soon as we got home, and I was not sorry to have the rest of the afternoon to think over Miss Nesmith's proposition, but, although I gave full weight to all the objections I could think of, none of them were sufficient to convince me I ought not to take the case.

When long after tea-time our friends came back in the highest spirits, I had to withstand, as best I could, the volleys of chaff that whistled about my ears. I got away from them immediately after tea, and reviewed the objections again, now that my first enthusiasm had cooled a little, but with the same result.

The next morning therefore I drove once more to the house in the wood, and told Miss Nesmith I had made up my mind to take the case. She was so much more grateful than I deserved that I felt obliged to tell her that any scientific man would give his eye-teeth for the chance of studying such a unique case, but all she said was: "I am glad there is anything to make your sacrifice lighter."

While we were talking over the details of the arrangement, she said:

"I shall be able to make you fairly comfortable, but the life will not be luxurious, as of course I can keep no servants, and, although the cooking and other hard work of the house are done by my farmer and his wife, there are many little things you will have to do for yourself."

"Oh," said I, "I am used to camping out, and shall enjoy that sort of picnic life."

Then I had an inspiration.

"Why not," said I, "introduce me to your brother as a man you have engaged to help in the work of the house? In this way we should get rid of our greatest difficulty—your brother's intense aversion to seeing a doctor; and I feel sure he will suspect nothing, if you tell him that I was a student a few years ago, and you hope may prove a pleasant companion for both of you."

At first she would not hear of any deceit—even such an innocent one—but when I pointed out to her that without it I saw no way of helping her brother, she very reluctantly agreed to carry out my plan.

This left, as far as I could see, only one difficulty, which was that, if her brother should recognize me as the cause of his last attack, he would refuse to have anything to do with me, but she assured me that one of these violent fits wiped out of his memory everything that happened during it, or for some time before, or afterwards.

I now went back to my quarters for the last time, told my fellow lodgers important business called me away, and I should not be able to take any more vacation that summer. The next morning I drove away in the direction of Boston, until I was out of sight, when I made the best of my way to the house in the wood.

There, following Miss Nesmith's directions, I drove to the farmhouse, which was hidden by a turn in the road, so that I had not seen it before, and left my horse and buggy with the farmer, who promised to take the greatest care of them.

This farm had belonged to the Nesmiths for generations, and the farmer and his wife were old family retainers and thoroughly trustworthy. Really, however, they knew little beyond the fact that Nesmith was insane, as he showed a morbid ingenuity in avoiding them, when they were working at the house, and his sister also did her best to keep him out of their way, since her experience with the doctor had made her realize fully the importance of secrecy.

I may as well explain here the reason for the extraordinary bolts, which fastened the gates in the fence, although I did not find it out till somewhat later. Nesmith was on his honor not to go outside the stockade, but, as he was unable to remember his promise when excited, he had himself contrived these bolts, which could not be shot in less than five minutes, as in that time he would be sure to remember, and not go out, even if he opened the gate.

I must say I felt decidedly nervous when Miss Nesmith introduced me to her brother as the man, who had come to help them with the work of the house, but I need not have worried myself about it, as it was plain he had not the least remembrance of having seen me before, and his surliness came only from his hatred of all strangers.

For some days I devoted myself to overcoming his dislike, and succeeded so well that in less than a week we were good friends; and I found him in his lucid intervals a pleasant sociable fellow; and soon became as anxious to cure him for his own sake as for his sister's.

While I was establishing these friendly relations with him, I began to study the case, and first read carefully the book which Miss Nesmith thought had put the idea of a double into his head just before his encounter with the jelly-fish. It was called "The Loyal Ronins," and was a translation of a novel by Tamenaga, the Japanese Dickens, made up of a collection of stories giving the experiences of the national heroes—the forty-seven ronins—while they were waiting until they should be able to avenge the death of their lord.

The story in question had to do with one of them named Sir Cliffside, who after a dreary winter in Yedo, where he had been sick as well as miserably poor, was made very happy by the arrival of his wife and children from Ako in charge of their devoted servant Original Help. Strangely enough this man was in every respect the very image of Sir Cliffside's servant also called Original Help, who had taken the greatest care of his master during that hard winter in Yedo, while the other Original Help was doing everything for the lady in Ako three hundred miles away. The ronin and his wife were thoroughly puzzled by this strange affair, until she said in a low terrified tone,—

"It is a case of the soul-dividing disease."

This disease is described in an ancient book called, "Prescriptions for Strange Sicknesses" as follows,— "If a person suddenly becomes two beings exactly resembling each other, it is a case of soul-dividing disease. You may know this by the fact of the duplicate person being unable to speak. The remedy for such an affliction is as follows:

"Take equal parts of gentian, asafoetida, and ginger, pound them in a mortar, and make a strong infusion. Give the person who can speak one *saké*-cupful every half hour. The medicine will make the patient bright and cheerful, and cause the duplicate wandering spirit to return to its proper body.

"This disease is a very rare one."

I also devoted some time to looking up the poisonous jellyfish—a most repulsive monster—which consists of a disc two feet or more across of a strangely corrugated jelly, that looks as if deeply tinged with clotted blood. Streamers or feelers twenty to thirty feet long and as fine as threads float out in all directions from the edge of the disc, and woe to the animal that comes against them, as it is instantly struck with paralysis.

Accidents to bathers from these frightful beasts are rare, because they live in deep water, and, when they drift into the zone of bathing, usually have been dead so long that they are nearly or quite harmless; and yet in the course of my study of these animals I learned that one of my most eminent colleagues had nearly lost his life in an encounter with one of them.

Naturally I had many talks with Miss Nesmith about the details of the case, and asked her with especial care whether the number of doubles had ever increased by more than one at a time. She was absolutely certain that there had never been an increase of more than one, and, when I suggested that she might have been too much excited to observe the number of doubles accurately, she assured me she had grown so thoroughly accustomed to their appearance that now she looked at them without the least excitement.

When I had made myself familiar with these details of the case, I tried exciting Nesmith, taking care, however, that he should not realize the excitement came from me; but my careful observation of his symptoms while he was throwing off doubles, led to only one discovery, and this seemed of slight importance. In the middle of his forehead a narrow scar continued the line of his nose up to his hair. It looked as if it had been made by the cut of a sharp knife, and usually was barely visible, but, when he was excited enough to throw off a double, it turned red, and grew so broad that no one could fail to notice it.

When later I increased the amount of excitement, so that he threw off several doubles at one time, the effect on the scar was very marked, as it grew into an angry red band more than an inch wide, and a slender white line appeared distinctly in the middle of it.

After three months of careful study I had mastered the facts of the case, and contrived a plan for curing my patient. Unfortunately it had to be a leap in the dark, as I could make no progress toward understanding the nature and cause of the disease, but I thought it over very carefully, and, after I had decided it was worth trying, I laid it before Miss Nesmith, who approved it although with a great deal of natural hesitation.

When all my preparations were complete, Miss Nesmith took refuge at the farmhouse, as I did not need her help, and the treatment I proposed to use would certainly be trying to her. Then I invited young Nesmith to my room, and he came eagerly, as I always had there something he liked such as a good cigar, or a box of chocolates; but this time, as soon as he was inside the door, I seized him by the throat, and forcing him against the wall, locked his wrists into a pair of handcuffs which I had fastened there above his head.

His frenzy was appalling, and he threw off at once a rush of doubles. As the first appeared I fired at it pointblank with a pistol I had ready. There was a moment of doubt and then—yes! Just as I had hoped, it dissolved and vanished before the bullet, as a wreath of mist melts before the wind.

After another shot had disposed of the second double in the same way, I felt confident of success, and yet amid the bewildering racket of the pistol shots and the frantic raving of the maniac, it was very hard to keep my head, and not miss my aim, or lose my count, but I went on grimly—three, four, five and I made no mistake, for with the removal of the sixth double my first revolver was empty. I snatched up a second that lay close at hand, and with this destroyed the seventh double, and the eighth, and then fired at the ninth, which I knew must come from such fierce excitement. As this last disappeared, I drew a sigh of relief, and was just laying down my pistol, when a tenth came gibbering and shrieking at me.

What was this?

Could he for the first time have thrown off two more doubles instead of one?

At any rate I must get rid of it. I raised my pistol, when—just as my finger was trembling on the trigger—I glanced through the powder smoke at the handcuffs on the wall.

They were empty!

The loss of all these doubles had reduced him so much that he had been able to draw his hands out of them, and I had nearly shot *her brother!*

Overcome with horror I threw the pistol as far from me as I could. With a yell of triumph the maniac pounced upon it, and made for me screaming and brandishing it in the air.

In such emergencies the mind works quickly. I remembered cases, in which raving lunatics had been controlled by the calmness of a bystander, and tried desperately to put on the needed calm and authority; but either I could not stop completely the trembling which was shaking me from head to foot, or his frenzy was too fierce to be controlled, for still he came on not quickly, but—what was worse—circling, or leaping from side to side in a slow deliberate advance.

At last the end came. He pushed the revolver against my temple, and I felt the hard circle of the steel pressing into my flesh. The jaws of the thing—bestial, or fiendish rather than human—were gnashing and slavering in my very face, while above them the scar—a sinister, dark, livid purple—encrusted his forehead from end to end, and the white line hung out from the midst of it, now a slender thread.

Driven by a sudden impulse I seized this thread, and, with a quick jerk tore it from his forehead.

The pistol dropped from his hand, and he fell, as if struck by lightning, but I caught him before he reached the floor, and dragged him to the bed. Then followed an anxious time, as I doubted if he could rally. I had been prepared for great exhaustion, but not for such an alarming collapse; and at first the powerful remedies I used had little or no effect, so it was a great relief, when I observed the first faint signs of returning life, still greater, when not long afterward I watched his stupor change into a natural sleep.

Now that the tension was relieved, I found I was tired—thoroughly tired—but soon I forgot all about that in the satisfaction of telling Miss Nesmith that all had gone well, and I had good hopes of a perfect cure; and I felt still more encouraged the next morning, when after sleeping twenty hours Nesmith woke up in even better condition than I had expected, and best of all showing no symptoms whatever of insanity. After this his progress was very rapid, and his recovery complete, so that the wildest excitement has never again been able to produce a trace of a double.

What did it all mean?

Some light was thrown on the subject by a microscopic examination of the thread torn from Nesmith's forehead, which showed it to be a piece of the streamer of a poisonous jellyfish, and it may

be that this caused an irritation, which spreading to the longitudi-
nal fissure of his brain made the two lobes act separately produc-
ing a twofold effect. Then, as his mind was full of the soul-dividing
disease, when it received that staggering blow, it would naturally
run on doubles, when it became unbalanced; but I do not care to
go further than this, for, although I have what seems to me a plau-
sible hypothesis to explain his translation of these vivid mental
pictures into the visible appearance of doubles, it rests on so many
uncertain suppositions that I doubt, if it would seem so convincing to anyone else.

Well! I got my fee; but I have never sent any account of this
remarkable case to the medical journals, as I was afraid my readers would find it hard to believe I was telling the truth, and I do
not care to publish such things about my wife's brother.

COACHWHIP PUBLICATIONS

COACHWHIPBOOKS.COM

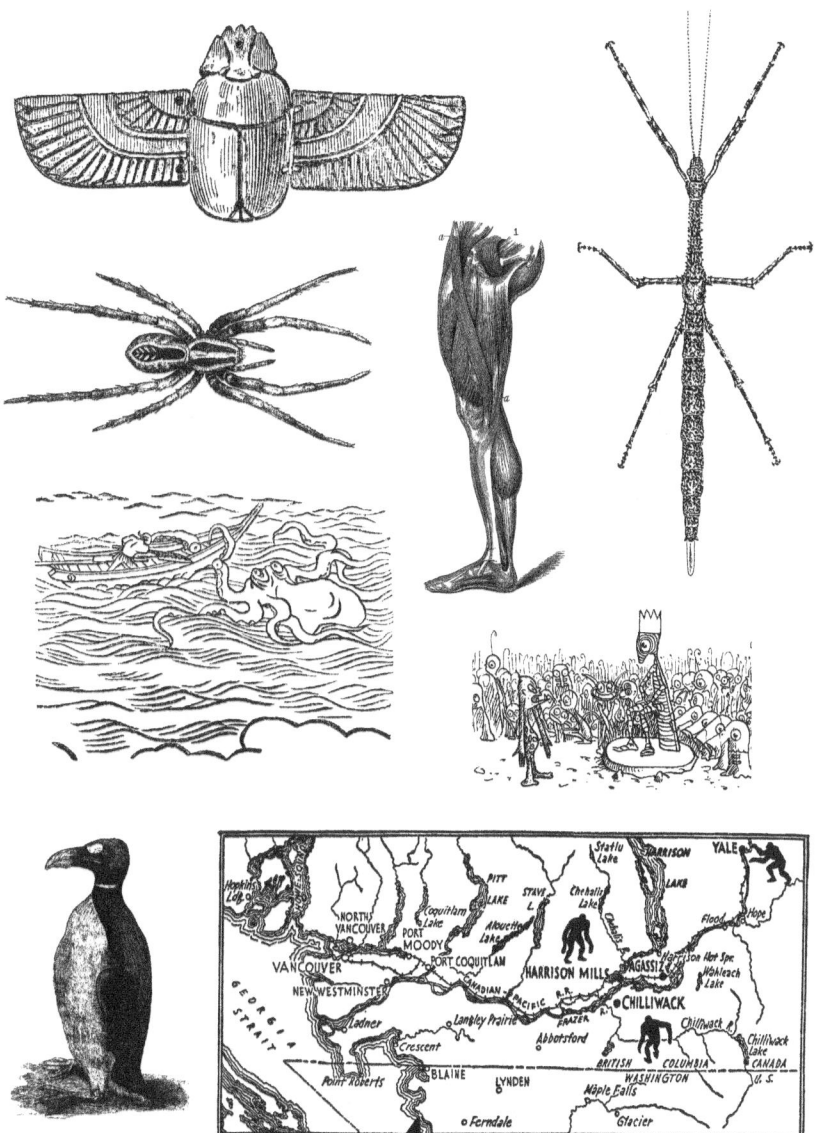

COACHWHIP PUBLICATIONS

COACHWHIPBOOKS.COM

Bestiarium Cryptozoologicum

Mystery Animals and Unknown Species
in Classic Science Fiction and Fantasy

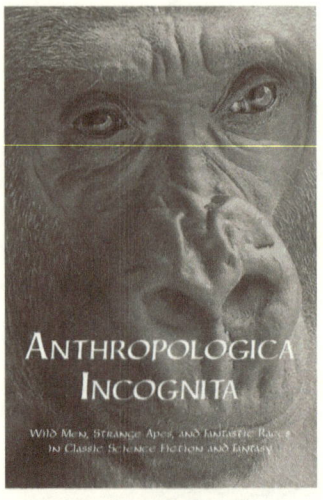

ANTHROPOLOGICA
INCOGNITA

Wild Men, Strange Apes, and Fantastic Races
in Classic Science Fiction and Fantasy

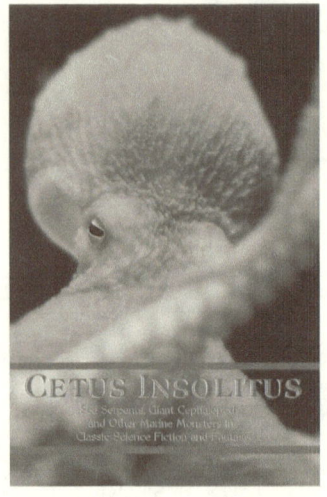

CETUS INSOLITUS

Sea Serpents, Giant Cephalopods,
and Other Marine Monsters in
Classic Science Fiction and Fantasy

INVERTEBRATA ENIGMATICA

Giant Spiders, Dangerous Insects, and other Strange Invertebrates
in Classic Science Fiction and Fantasy

Unknown Creatures and Monstrous Beasts
in Classic Science Fiction and Fantasy

COACHWHIP PUBLICATIONS

ALSO AVAILABLE

Flora Curiosa
ISBN 1-930585-56-X

COACHWHIP PUBLICATIONS

COACHWHIPBOOKS.COM

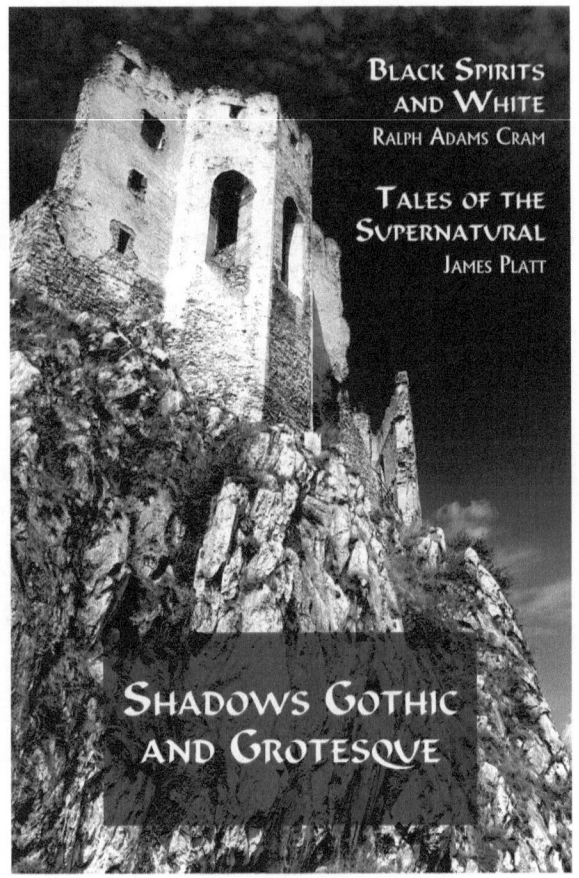

Shadows Gothic and Grotesque
ISBN 1-61646-059-8

H. G. Wells:
Tales of the Weird and Supernatural
ISBN 1-61646-072-5

www.ingramcontent.com/pod-product-compliance
Lightning Source LLC
Chambersburg PA
CBHW051256250626
47155CB00009B/3315